GIRL V THE WORLD

Sophie Bennett Saves the Planet

hardie grant EGMONT

Sophie Bennett Saves the Planet
published in 2013 by
Hardie Grant Egmont
Ground Floor, Building 1, 658 Church Street
Richmond, Victoria 3121, Australia
www.hardiegrantegmont.com.au

A CiP record for this title is available from the National Library of Australia.

Text copyright © 2013 Meredith Badger
Illustration and design copyright © 2013 Hardie Grant Egmont

Design by Michelle Mackintosh
Text design and typesetting by Ektavo

Printed in Australia by Griffin Press, an Accredited ISO AS/NZS
14001:2004 Environmental Management System printer.

1 3 5 7 9 10 8 6 4 2

The paper this book is printed on is certified against the
Forest Stewardship Council® Standards. Griffin Press holds
FSC chain of custody certification SGS-COC-005088. FSC
promotes environmentally responsible, socially beneficial
and economically viable management of the world's forests.

Sophie Bennett Saves the Planet

Meredith Badger

hardie grant EGMONT

One

It's Sunday afternoon and I'm riding towards the local pool to meet my friends Leni and Anya. The pool reopened for the season a couple of weeks ago, but this is the first day that it's been hot enough to go. It seems like everyone is outside today, enjoying the sunshine. Everyone except me, that is. Hot weather makes me worry, and not just because of sunburn – although with my pale skin that's always likely. It's because of something my parents always say. When everyone else is joyfully chucking on their T-shirts and sandals, my parents are shaking their heads and saying,

'It shouldn't be so warm at this time of year.'

Global warming. That's one of the things I worry about a lot. I worry about it because climate change is affecting the environment. Wet places are getting drier. Cool places are getting warmer. And animals have fewer and fewer places to live. That's on top of all the other stuff they have to cope with, like pollution and forests being cut down.

So that's a little glimpse into the brain of Sophie Bennett. Strange, huh? Most thirteen-year-old girls I know worry about stuff like what they should wear on the casual-clothes day at school. Or whether some hot guy likes them. As far as I know, I'm the only thirteen-year-old who finds it hard to enjoy a sunny spring day because she's thinking about what happens to frogs when their lake disappears.

I blame it on my parents. They're obsessed with this sort of stuff. Mum works as a wildlife rescuer, which means that people call her if they've found a koala wandering down the middle of the main street (it happens) or a lizard with a broken leg. We often look after these animals at home. Last week, for instance, we had a wombat wandering around.

When they're ready, Mum releases the animals back

into the wild. I know she often worries about what will happen to them next. I mean, it keeps her up at night. Which is probably why when she's not working, she's busy going to rallies and demonstrations to make people aware of climate change and to pressure governments to do something about it.

Dad's job has nothing to do with animals or nature – he works in IT – but he does a lot of campaigning too and knows heaps about the environment. Actually, he knows heaps about everything. He's always got about twenty books out from the library at once.

'Knowledge makes you powerful, Soph,' my dad says to me sometimes. I get what he means. But sometimes, like on days like today when everyone else is happy about the sunshine and I have a knot in my stomach about it, I can't help thinking how much easier it'd be not to know so much. Sometimes knowledge makes you lonely.

I wheel my bike around to the left and take a shortcut through the skate park. Lots of people from school hang out there, especially Edi Rhineheart and Hazel Atherton because they go out with two of the boys who practically live there – Archie de Souza and his friend Leo Flynn. There's hardly anyone here today, though, at the skate park.

As I near the ramp I check out the graffiti to see if anything's changed. My favourite piece is still there. It's of a girl in a bikini wearing a beauty-queen sash that says 'Miss Everything'. For some reason, the girl has these huge feet, and underneath there's a caption: 'Filling the Big Shoes'. I'm pretty sure it was done by Leo and I wonder if it's supposed to be his girlfriend, Hazel. Or maybe it's Edi. But Edi's feet are definitely not large. Edi's feet are perfect, like the rest of her. I guess it's the 'everything' bit that makes me think of her. She's got what a lot of people at school want. Brains. Beauty. A boyfriend. Dad told me once that good art is something that makes you think and this picture definitely does that. It's very cool. I'd love to tell Leo one day how much I like it, but he's in the year above us at school and I'm pretty sure he doesn't know I exist.

When I arrive at the pool I realise why no-one was at the park. Everyone is here. The concrete car park is super hot and I feel the heat radiating up towards me as I push my bike over to the rack. There are a couple of boys there, chaining up their own bikes. One of them sniggers when he sees mine.

'Man. What century did that thing come from?'

Hardly any of the stuff I own is new. It's not that we're poor exactly, it's just that my parents don't go out and *buy* stuff like most people. My mum is big on op shops and trash-and-treasure finds and my dad loves fixing things up. A bit of glue. A bit of paint. 'Giving it a new lease on life,' he calls it. This sounds nice, I guess, but what it means is that my things always look different to everyone else's. Which means that *I* always look different to everyone else.

Take my bike, for instance. Dad found it one evening in the hard rubbish and brought it home. He was so pleased with it. 'It has a great, solid frame. It'll last for twenty years once I've redone the brakes.' He fixed up the gears too. Mum wrapped ribbons around the handlebars and painted orange-and-purple swirls over the rusty spots on the frame. When they presented it to me they were both so thrilled that I couldn't turn around and say, 'I hate it. It's ugly.'

They would've been shattered. So instead I said, 'Wow! Thanks!' and steeled myself for the rude comments I knew would be coming my way when I turned up at school on this thing.

Luckily my friend Anya has taught me how to deal with dumb remarks – or at least, I picked up some tricks from watching her. Anya is very good at turning an insult into a joke. Sometimes I think she does it a bit too much – she puts herself down a bit – but it is a pretty good trick.

I turn to the sniggering boy and shrug my shoulders. 'Hey, this bike is cutting-edge compared to the penny-farthing I used to ride,' I say.

He gapes at me. It doesn't matter that he probably has no idea what a penny-farthing is. All that matters is that it shuts him up for long enough for me to walk off. I don't bother locking my bike. That's the one good thing about having *pre-loved* stuff. Generally people don't want to steal it.

There's a long queue to get into the pool and just as I'm finally pushing through the turnstiles, there's a message from Anya.

Where R U?

Anya is the texting queen. She'll text you when she's standing two people ahead of you in the queue for the school canteen. She'll text you when you go to the loo during a movie night. I'm not so big on it myself. For one thing, my phone is ancient (of course) and the predictive text doesn't work so it takes me ages to write anything. I don't bother replying. I figure it'll be way quicker if I just go and get changed and hurry to meet them.

In the change room I pull on my bathers. They're a one-piece. There's no way Mum would let me wear a bikini and, to be honest, I wouldn't want to wear one anyway. I'd feel way too self-conscious. I actually like my bathers. My aunt Kaye gave them to me for my birthday and they're brand-new. Next I slather on the SPF 50 sunscreen. Anything less and I'll look like a cocktail sausage in twenty minutes flat.

'*There* you are, Soph!' It's Anya standing in the entrance to the change room, her hands on her hips. She's wearing a bikini and she clearly doesn't feel one little bit self-conscious about it. 'Leni's out there with the guys, minding our spot,' Anya says.

My insides sort of skid sideways when she says that, like I've taken a corner too fast on my bike. By *the guys* Anya means Leni's mates from athletics training: Adam and Josh. Adam hangs around with us a lot and it's pretty obvious he's got a *thing* for Leni. I always figured that Josh got dragged along without having much say in it. But just recently, this crazy thought has come into my head. One that's so crazy I would die rather than tell anyone about it. Even my friends. Recently I've been wondering if Josh has been hanging around because of *me*.

One part of me thinks that this is totally ridiculous. But then another part keeps looking for clues that maybe he *does* like me. I sometimes feel as if I have this gauge in my head – one of those things with a needle that swings from one side to the other. Sometimes when Josh is around, the needle swings towards 'He likes you'. But other times it goes straight over to 'You're imagining things, Sophie Bennett'.

Anya taps her foot impatiently as I put my bag in a locker. 'Hurry *up*, Soph!' she says.

I quickly check that I've got everything. Towel. Hat. Sunscreen. Water bottle. Right. I'm ready for anything.

'Okay,' I say. 'Let's go.'

The pool smells like chlorine, sunscreen and lemonade iceblocks. Everywhere I look, I see someone I know. Erin and George are on the grass near the change rooms, deep in conversation about something – probably some computer game, knowing those two. Briana and Phoebe are nearby, flicking through magazines.

Sitting on the edge of the pool, chatting as they dangle their legs in the water, are Edi, Hazel and their boyfriends Archie and Leo. The four of them look like they're in a poster advertising summer.

Anya calls out hi to them and I have to admit I cringe a bit. It's not like we're friends with them. But of course in Anya's perfect dream world, everyone would be friends with everyone. Perfect Edi would hang out with the girl on the orange-and-purple pre-loved bike.

Four heads turn in our direction. Four smiles pass across us and away, like lighthouse beams. Then the poster kids turn their attention back towards each other.

Near the kiosk is this loser guy called Nelson who is the year above us at school. He's hard to miss at the best of times because he's big and loud but today he's especially hard to ignore. He's standing on the path, his arm draped around a blonde girl, and as we walk past, he pretty much shoves his tongue down her throat right in front of us. It's completely disgusting and I can't imagine what this girl is *thinking*, letting Nelson go anywhere near her.

Earlier in the year someone wrote this 'hot list' ranking the girls in our year in order of 'hotness'. It was pinned up on a noticeboard. No-one knows for sure who did it but most people suspect it was Nelson. I was way down on the list, and I guess I was supposed to feel cut about that, but actually I just felt creeped out that someone had *rated* me – especially someone like Nelson Cooke. If I was making a list of the hottest boys (and I never would), he wouldn't even be in the top one hundred. Not even the top million.

Leni was in the bottom half of the list too, which just shows how dumb it was because she's gorgeous. Anya was in the top twenty and although she said she was disgusted, I think she was a tiny bit flattered.

I hate how those ratings have stuck in people's heads, even though the list was ripped up. Things like that never properly disappear, that's the problem. That's why it's always bugged me that the person who did it never got into trouble.

'Leni's over there,' says Anya, pointing. I can see Leni over on the grassy area on the other side of the pool. Adam and Josh are with her and they've got a ball, which they're throwing back and forth between them. Josh looks up and smiles as we get close. The gauge in my head swings over – just a little – to the 'like' side.

'Uh, excuse me? We're at the swimming pool, not the football field, you know!' Anya calls out.

Adam has Leni in a headlock and Anya rushes over to 'save' her, although I can tell she's secretly hoping he'll do the same thing to her. Adam is definitely very cute, but lately I've been thinking Josh is better looking.

Anya and I sit down on the concrete and Leni, Adam and Josh come to join us. I notice that Josh chooses a spot next to me, even though there's a much bigger space next to Adam. My imaginary gauge needle moves a fraction more into 'like'.

'Wow, Soph,' says Anya suddenly. 'Your legs are *so* white!'

I look at them and sigh. 'Yeah, kind of dazzling, aren't they?'

'Don't worry about it,' says Josh. 'White is better than leathery any day.' As he says this an old couple with skin exactly like leather walk past and it's very, very hard not to laugh.

The conversation turns to favourite TV shows, which inevitably leads to *Acacia Lane*. It's one of those shows that everyone either loves or hates. Anya completely loves it. She got Leni hooked and because Leni watches it, Adam does too.

Josh grunts in disgust and looks at me. 'Please tell me you don't watch that stupid show too, Soph.'

I laugh and shake my head. 'We don't have a TV,' I say.

Josh looks surprised, as everyone does when they find this out.

'We've got a computer, though, so I watch DVDs on it sometimes,' I say quickly, but I can see the damage is done. It's one more thing to add to the list of weird stuff about me. I sometimes feel like I should walk around holding up a sign that says 'DIFFERENT' in huge, red letters. Underneath could be a whole lot of check boxes.

Rides an ugly bike.

Wears strange clothes.

Doesn't have a TV.

Doesn't eat meat.

'Wow!' says Josh. 'I've never met anyone without a TV before.'

The 'like' gauge screeches over to 'You're imagining things'.

Leni, who can never sit still for very long, jumps to her feet. 'Time for a swim,' she says, and two seconds later neatly dives into the nearest pool.

Josh looks at me and Anya. 'What about you two?'

Anya goes to the edge of the pool, dips a toe into the water, then quickly pulls it out again. 'There's no way I'm going in there,' she declares. 'It's freezing!'

I see Josh and Adam exchange a look – a mischievous one. Before Anya can step away, the two of them run up to her, grabbing her under the arms as they jump in. Anya tumbles in, screaming at the top of her lungs.

'Come on, Soph!' calls Leni, her wet hair flicking over her shoulder. 'It's great once you're in.'

'No, it's not!' calls Anya, surfacing. But she's looking pretty happy, even though her hair has stuck down against her head.

Adam attempts to dunk Leni but she manages to wiggle away. 'Come *on*, Soph!' she says. 'We need you in here.'

'Okay, okay,' I say. 'I'm coming.' I run to the edge of the pool and leap in.

Afterwards, Josh and Adam go to the kiosk for snacks and Leni, Anya and I stretch out on the concrete to warm up. I lie on my back with my arms out to the sides like a T, eyes closed against the sun. But then a shadow falls across my face and I open my eyes again. Nelson is standing there, one arm still around the blonde girl and a stupid smile on his face.

'Check out the hairy pits on this chick!' he says, pointing at my underarms. He says it really loudly and it suddenly feels like everyone in the entire pool is staring is me. I'm too shocked to do anything besides jam my arms against my sides. But Anya leaps into action.

'Shut up, Nelson, you moron!' she snaps. For a small person, Anya can yell very loudly. 'No-one cares what you think so just get lost.'

Nelson looks like he's planning on hanging around but Adam and Josh come back, holding iceblocks and cans of drink.

'What's going on?' says Josh. Josh is not a big talker, but he's got this way of sounding very serious and like you wouldn't want to mess with him. Also, although he's younger than Nelson, he's almost as big.

'Nothing,' mumbles Nelson and slinks off with the girl.

'What was all that about?' asks Adam, passing out iceblocks.

'Nothing. Just Nelson being a jerk,' says Leni. I'm grateful to her for not telling the guys what happened, but I'm also feeling pretty shaken up. And really self-conscious too. Of course I'd noticed that I'd started to sprout a bit of under-arm hair, but it was so little that I didn't really pay much attention. Most of the time it's covered up. I just totally forgot that in my bathers it would be visible. But even if I *had* thought about it before coming to the pool, what would I have done? I've never shaved before, or anything like that.

The unwrapped iceblock is beginning to soften in my hand, but I don't feel like eating it. What I feel like doing is getting dressed and going home. I'm looking over towards the change rooms when I notice something under a nearby tree. I think at first it's a fluffy brown hat or a curled up scarf, but when I go over I realise that it's a ringtail possum.

Maybe it's hurt, I think, but although it's still warm, it's not moving at all.

'Gross, Soph! It's dead. Leave it alone.' My friends have gathered around me, although Anya is hanging way back with a disgusted expression on her face.

'I'm just checking if it's a female. Maybe it's got a baby in its pouch,' I say. This is something my mum always does if we see dead wildlife. She'll even pull over if we're in the car, so doing this doesn't seem strange to me.

The possum is a female and when I check the pouch there's a curled-up little ball of fur in there. I gently scoop it out.

Leni inches forward. 'Is it dead?' she says.

The furball is warm and I can see – just faintly – its side lifting and falling.

'No, it's alive, but it's probably dehydrated,' I say. I take the baby possum over to my towel and gently wrap it up, making sure that air can still get through. 'I'd better take it to Mum straight away.'

Adam whistles and shakes his head. 'You are one gutsy chick, Soph. I can't believe you just did that.' I know he means it as a compliment but it's no big deal to me. I can't imagine *not* doing it.

I get changed quickly and say goodbye to my friends.

'Hey, good luck,' says Josh. 'I hope you make it back in time.' He's got a strange look on his face. Like seeing me remove that baby possum has made him think about me in a different way. I'm just not sure if it's in a *good* way or not. My 'like' gauge returns to the middle. Just as it always does.

Three

Dad and Mum built our house themselves. It's made out of straw – just like the first little pig's house – but you can't tell because the strawbale is all hidden away behind a layer of mud. Our house stands out in the street because it is so different-looking, but I love it anyway. It reminds me of a burrow or a cave because it's cosy and warm inside. We have a huge garden, too, with lots of trees and a vegie patch.

I leave my bike in the front yard, pick up the baby possum still bundled in the towel and hurry inside. There's no-one in the house but I can hear voices drifting up from the backyard – Mum's and Dad's and also a third voice. I give a little inward groan because I know who this has to be: our next-door neighbour, Daphne.

The house next to ours has had a steady stream of people moving in and out over the years. So many that I stopped paying attention to who they were. The latest lot are the Mitchells, Daphne and her three kids: two little boys and a girl called Eliza who's a year above me at school. Pretty much from the moment they moved in, Daphne was over at our house, chewing my mum's ear off and getting my dad to fix stuff for her.

I don't understand why my parents like Daphne so much. She's the last person you'd expect them to be friends with. She drives a big car that must use heaps of petrol, she dumps all her rubbish in the same bin instead of separating it, and the TV is always on so loudly at her place that you can hear it from ours. But instead of marching over there and telling her to turn it off, which is what I'd expect my parents to do, Mum and Dad just close the window. Weird.

Dad once told me that there was this woman in Greek mythology called Daphne who was turned into a tree – and my parents are very big on trees. That's about the only thing they can have in common. But Daphne seems less like a tree and more like one of those weeds always trying to take over. What my mum calls an 'invasive species'. She's always asking my parents these super-personal questions, like, 'Why aren't you married?', 'Why don't you eat meat?' and 'How do you manage without a car?' It makes me squirm, but my parents don't seem to mind at all. When I ask Mum about it, all she says is, 'Daphne's got a good heart, love.'

Deep inside the towel I feel the possum stir. I take a deep breath. Go outside.

Mum and Daphne are sitting on the back steps, drinking coffee. As they're sitting there together, I can't help comparing the way they look. Daphne sounds like an old person's name but she's younger than my parents. My parents *are* kind of old, though – Mum was forty when she had me and Dad was forty-five. They say they were too busy before then. Sometimes I wonder if they meant to have me at all. Maybe I was an accident.

Daphne looks totally different to my mum too. She

has long blonde hair and she's always really made-up, with blusher and everything. I've never seen her wear any shoes other than high heels, even on the weekend. My mum *never* wears high heels and she hardly ever puts on make-up. She's had dreadlocks for years and they're pretty much completely grey. I've seen pictures of Mum when she was in her twenties and she had this beautiful long brown hair. Sometimes I wish she'd get rid of the dreads and dye it back to that colour. It'd make her look way younger. But I already know what she'd say if I suggested it. Hair dye is full of polluting chemicals and anyway, she's not ashamed of having grey hair. 'You can't stop getting older, love. So why pretend to be something that you're not?'

See why I find her friendship with Daphne so weird?

'Hi, love!' says Mum as I walk over and give her a kiss. 'How was the human soup today?'

'Human *soup?*' repeats Daphne.

Mum laughs. 'I mean the swimming pool.'

But there are more important things to talk about right now than the pool. I hold out the towel bundle to Mum. 'I found a baby possum,' I tell her. 'I think it's dehydrated.'

Mum swings into animal-rescue mode. We take the bundle into the kitchen where Mum carefully unwraps it. Daphne hangs in the background.

'Oh, you're just a tiny girl, aren't you?' Mum croons when the big-eyed baby is revealed. 'Don't worry, Poss. We'll get you a drink.' She fills a pipette with some sterilised water and offers it to the possum, who looks unsure at first, but then sucks a few drops down. I feel myself relax a little. It's a good sign if it's drinking.

'Should I mix up some possum formula?' I ask her.

'There's a special formula just for possums?' Daphne says.

'Of course!' says Mum. 'Possums are lactose intolerant so cow's milk is no good.' She smiles at me. 'Sure, that'd be great, Soph. It'll be good for Poss to have some later, once she's rehydrated a bit. I'll call Julie and see if she can look after her.'

'But can't *we* look after her?' I say, surprised.

Dad wanders into the kitchen then, holding a bright purple laptop. It has to be Daphne's. He and Mum exchange a look. There's something going on and I can tell from her expression that even Daphne knows about it.

'Honey,' says Mum. She's using the same voice she uses for injured animals. Calm and gentle. 'You know how Dad is going away for a couple of days with that forest action group to set up their computer network?'

I nod. It's not the first time Dad has gone and helped an environmental group with their technology stuff. But I don't see what this has to do with Poss.

'Well, they rang today and asked if I could possibly come too,' Mum continues. 'They want to train up some of their members in the basics of rescuing injured wildlife. I said I'd talk to you about it. It would mean I'd have to leave tonight, with Dad. But we'd be back on Saturday morning.'

It's still really sunny, but I suddenly feel cold. 'And what would happen to me? Would I be here alone?'

I see Mum's eyes flick over to Daphne and I suddenly guess what they've cooked up.

'Daphne's very kindly offered to have you stay at her house for the week,' Mum says.

Everyone looks at me expectantly.

'I really don't want you to go,' I say. But Mum must have known I'd say that.

'It's just a week, love,' she says.

I think quickly. 'What about the rally next weekend?'

'We'd be back for the rally,' she says. 'But it's okay, Soph. If you really want me to stay, I will.'

Then Dad joins in. 'Well, let's discuss it a bit more, shall we?'

Daphne coughs and stands up. 'I'd better head home,' she says. 'The boys are probably tearing the place apart by now.' Then she smiles at me. 'If you change your mind, you're more than welcome to come and stay with us. And the possum too, if you like.' Then she goes and I hear her heels clacking down our front path.

Mum looks at me hopefully. 'Daphne said you can take Poss,' she says. 'Does that make any difference?'

I shake my head. 'No. It'd be dangerous for Poss at her place. Those little boys are maniacs.'

Mum puts up her hands. 'Okay,' she says. 'I won't ask again.' She gets up and walks into another room, leaving me in the kitchen with Dad.

Dad starts washing up the coffee mugs. He always thinks a lot before he says anything and I can feel him thinking right now. I know it'll be about letting Mum go. But I'm not going to back down on this. There's no way I'm staying next door.

'Your mum is really good at what she does, Soph,' Dad says after a few minutes. I know this, of course, and I'm proud of her. 'But there's only so many animals she can help,' Dad goes on. 'She can't be everywhere, all the time.'

Poss accepts another couple of water droplets from the pipette. She'll be ready for some milk soon. And then I think about how if it wasn't for Mum teaching me how to take care of animals, Poss would probably be dead by now.

There's still a part of me that wants to say, 'Can't someone else teach them? Why does it have to be *my* mum?' But I know this isn't fair. I bundle Poss back up in the towel and go and find Mum.

'Mum?' I say. 'Can I borrow the pet carrier for Poss? I'll need it if I'm going to take her with me to Daphne's.'

Mum's face glows with delight. 'Really? Are you sure, Soph?'

'Yeah, I'm sure,' I say. I even manage a smile.

Mum puts her arm around me, careful to avoid squashing Poss. 'Thanks, love. It means a lot.'

V

The next half-hour is a frantic rush to get everything packed. I fling some stuff into my school bag – uniform, socks, undies, PJs. I grab supplies for Poss too and I find the special fur-lined pouch that Mum keeps small animals in, which you can wear around your neck.

It happens so fast that I can't quite believe it when the taxi arrives to take my parents to the bus station. We take all our stuff outside and when Mum hugs me, I can tell she's having doubts.

'Are you sure you're okay with this, Soph?' she says. 'You won't get homesick?'

'Of course she won't,' says Dad. He bends to hug me too and whispers in my ear, 'I'm proud of you, honey.'

I start to choke up but I swallow it down. 'Thanks, Dad,' I gulp.

I stand and wave until the taxi has gone. Then I sling my bag on my shoulder, pick up the pet carrier (which is empty, because I have Poss in the pouch) with one hand and grab my bike with the other. Then I slowly wheel my bike over to Daphne's house.

Four

Daphne's place is about as different to ours as she is to my mum. It's sort of like a huge doll's house. It's big and fancy, but there's something not very solid about it, like if you gave it a push the whole thing would fall down. And while we have a really big, lush garden that my parents spend all their free time in, Daphne's yard just has a couple of scraggly bushes and a metal shed. The rest is mostly concrete. I lean my bike against the side of the house and go and ring the doorbell.

When Daphne opens the door, it's like I've been hit in

the face by a sledgehammer of noise. Every single gadget in the entire house seems to be on maximum volume. To top it off, the two boys are running around yelling at each other. I feel Poss burrow down deeper into the pouch.

'Thomas, stop chasing your little brother with the fly-swatter. He's a boy, not a bug. And Oscar, stop screaming!' Daphne calls over her shoulder. Then she beckons to me. 'Come in, Soph! I'm so glad you decided to stay with us!'

'Thanks for having me,' I mumble as I walk in.

I suddenly remember something Dad said to me once. *When I'm somewhere I don't want to be, I pretend to be an anthropologist — someone who studies humans. I watch the way people act and behave. It turns it into a game.* I decide to give it a go.

If the outside of Daphne's place is empty, then the inside definitely makes up for it. There's stuff everywhere. Toys. Clothes. There's a huge pile of junk mail on a coffee table in the lounge room. *This tribe likes to hoard printed materials,* I think, in anthropologist mode.

'Eliza! Sophie's here!' says Daphne to the couch and it's only then that I see Eliza lying there, reading a magazine and eating chips. I decide I'd better make an effort. After all, I'm going to be here for six nights.

'Hey, Eliza,' I say. 'Thanks for letting me stay.'

'Hi,' Eliza grunts back without even looking up.

I make another mental note. *The teenage female avoids eye contact.*

'Let's put your stuff away,' says Daphne. She takes my schoolbag and leads me up the hallway, her heels clopping on the wooden boards. She stops in front of a closed door. 'Eliza's really excited about having you share with her,' Daphne says. I seriously doubt this is true. The door may as well have a 'Keep Out' sign on it.

I'd suspected that Eliza and I had nothing in common, and her room proves me right. From the band posters stuck on the walls to the TV beside her desk, nothing in there is anything like *me*. I think about my own room, with my books and the rainforest mural Mum's friend Julie painted on the wall. On Eliza's floor is an inflatable mattress with a faded Barbie doona lying across it. Daphne must've been pretty confident I'd change my mind about coming to stay.

'I'll leave you to settle in,' says Daphne. 'Do you need

anything for the – ah – pup? I mean, what do you call a baby possum?'

'A joey,' I say. 'But thanks, I have everything I need.'

I take out my PJs and put them on my bed. There's no room for any of my other things so I just leave them in my bag. I look longingly at the book I brought, wishing I could lie here quietly and read it for a while, but that would probably be rude. So slowly, reluctantly, I head back to the lounge room.

V

The boys have started fighting. *Really* fighting. The smaller one, Oscar, has the bigger one, Thomas, around the waist and Thomas is clonking Oscar on the head with his fist. Oscar is yelling, 'I hate you! I hate you!' and Thomas is screaming, 'I hate you more!' It's horrible. People are always feeling sorry for me because I'm an only child, but right now siblings don't look so great to me.

'Boys!' says Daphne, running in from another room to break them apart. 'Behave yourselves. We have a guest.'

They both stop and stare at me. 'She's not a guest,' says Oscar. 'She's just the girl from next door. The one with the funny bike.'

'Sophie *is* our guest for the next few days,' says Daphne.

'Why?' asks Thomas. They are both staring at me curiously and I feel myself go from being the anthropologist to the person being studied.

'Because her parents have gone away for a couple of days,' explains Daphne. 'They've gone to help some people save a forest.'

'Why do they want to save a *forest*?' says Thomas, his nose wrinkled. 'Forests are just trees, and trees are dumb.'

'They're not dumb,' I tell him. 'Trees produce oxygen. That's the stuff we breathe. If there are no trees then there's no oxygen and then we all die.' Okay, so maybe that's simplifying things a bit, but at least it shuts the little twerp up. Both of them, actually.

There's a ringing noise from the kitchen.

'Ah, the oven timer!' Daphne says, clopping off towards the sound. 'Dinner's ready, guys!'

The boys run to the couch and reach for the remote.

But Daphne grabs it first and whisks it away. 'No,' she says. 'Tonight we're going to sit together at the table.'

'Why?' says Eliza, from the couch.

'Because that's what you do when you have a guest,' says Daphne.

Three sets of eyes turn to me and glare. Oh great. Now I'm the dinner-wrecker too.

Dinner is pizza and salad. When Daphne serves me a slice, I notice little pink cubes on it. Ham. But I'm not about to create any more fuss, so I start discreetly picking the ham bits off and hiding them under a lettuce leaf. Then Daphne spots me, and slaps her hands to her face.

'Oh, I'm *so* sorry, Sophie!' she says. 'I forgot you're vegetarian. I'll go and find you something else.' She starts to get up but I hastily stop her.

'No, it's okay,' I say. 'I've got all the ham off now.'

'Well, there's plenty of salad at least,' says Daphne.

'Yes,' I agree. I don't tell her that the salad tastes strange to me. Sort of like plastic. I guess I'm used to the salads at home, where most of the ingredients come straight from our garden.

'Why don't you eat ham?' asks Thomas.

'Because I love animals too much to eat them,' I tell him. It's my standard answer.

Thomas laughs. 'Ham doesn't come from *animals*,' he says. 'Ham comes from the supermarket.'

'Ham is made from a pig, dummy,' says Eliza. It's the most I've heard her say since I arrived.

'Don't call your brother a dummy, Eliza,' says Daphne. 'But yes, Thomas. Ham comes from pigs.'

'I'm eating a *pig?*' says Thomas, staring at his pizza slice in surprise.

'Yep. A tasty, tasty pig,' says Eliza. She takes a big bite of pizza and looks at me, like she's hoping I might burst into tears or something.

I can't wait for this meal to be over so I can go and feed Poss. She's starting to get restless in her pouch, which I've hidden on my lap under the table.

'I know! Let's play a game,' says Daphne suddenly. 'Let's tell each other about the best thing that happened to us today.'

Eliza groans. 'Mum! No!'

'Oh, come on,' says Daphne. 'It'll be fun! I'll start.' She taps her chin with her finger before saying, 'The best thing for me about today was opening the front door and seeing Sophie standing there.'

The boys go next. They have the same best thing – winning on Wii Super Mario Galaxy Adventure. But then they get into an argument about whether Oscar did actually win or not.

'What about you, Sophie?' says Daphne. 'What's the best thing that happened today?'

Best to just get this over with, I decide. I wonder if Daphne's hoping I'll say, *Finding out I was coming to stay with you guys!* But there's no way I'm saying that. 'Meeting my friends at the swimming pool,' I say. And it *was* good, especially if I block out the Nelson stuff.

Daphne beams. 'How lovely!' she says, clearly thrilled that I've gone along with her game. 'Now it's your turn, Eliza.'

Eliza slouches down into her seat and rolls her eyes. 'There was no best bit,' she says. 'Just lots of worst bits.' I can *tell* that me being here is one of them.

'Oh, come on, Lize,' pleads her mum. 'Tell us the *least-bad* bit then.'

Eliza sighs and starts to speak in a bored monotone. 'The least-bad bit was talking with Nelson this morning and arranging to meet up with him in the afternoon –'

She's cut off by the boys, who start up a sing-songy rhyme. 'Lizie's got a boyfriend. Lizie's got a boyfriend.'

Daphne quietens them. 'Go on, Lize.'

'But that,' continues Eliza, 'turned bad because Nelson had to cancel, because he forgot he had soccer practice.'

To be honest, I'm not sure if I'm getting this right. 'Are you going out with Nelson Cooke?' I say.

Eliza's eyes fix on me. 'Yep,' she says. 'Why?'

Personally, I'd want to know if my supposed boyfriend had been at the swimming pool all afternoon snogging some other girl. To me, the truth is important. Really important, even if it hurts. Because if you don't know the truth, how can anything feel real? But I also know that not everyone thinks like this. 'I just didn't know that,' I say, lamely.

Finally dinner ends and I start cleaning up. It's just

automatic because it's what I do at home. But Daphne acts like I've sprouted wings and started to float. 'How kind of you, Sophie,' she says. 'Eliza, could you help? That way I can get the boys bathed at a reasonable hour for once.'

Eliza shoots me yet another dirty look. Seriously, I can't do anything right.

We take the dishes to the kitchen and start cleaning up in silence. Eventually Eliza flicks on the radio and I start humming along.

Eliza looks at me. 'Do you actually know any of these songs?' she says.

'Well, no,' I admit. 'But they're not that complicated to pick up.'

Eliza does one of her lovely snorts and shakes her head. Frankly, I'm getting a little tired of Eliza's snorts and eye-rolls and glares.

I dump the tea towel I'm holding and put my hands on my hips. 'What?'

'It's just that you're so incredibly weird,' says Eliza. 'Everyone at school thinks so. Do you know that?'

Of course I know. I'm the one who has to turn up every

day on a bike decorated with ribbons, after all. I'm the one who never has the right brand of runners for sport. I'm the one whose lunch is a daily joke. But right now I've had about as much as I'm prepared to take from Eliza.

'Do you want to know what *I* think is really weird?' I say. 'I think it's really weird that Nelson Cooke was at the pool this afternoon, kissing some girl who was definitely not *you*.'

Eliza freezes, an empty pizza box in her hand. 'I don't believe it,' she says. She sounds like there's something stuck in her throat. 'You're just making it up.'

Straight away I feel bad. *Terrible*. I pick up the tea towel and get busy drying an already-dry plate. 'Well, maybe I made a mistake,' I mumble. But I can't look at her because I know I didn't make a mistake and I'm terrible at lying.

Daphne comes in just then. 'The boys are squeaky clean and I've promised them dessert,' she says in that chirpy way of hers. 'Do you girls feel like some ice-cream?'

Eliza shakes her head robotically. 'I don't feel well,' she says. 'I'm going to bed.' Then she runs out of the room, head down, and a moment later her bedroom door clicks closed.

Daphne looks at me, surprised. 'I wonder what's wrong with her?' she says.

I pick up the pizza box Eliza dropped so I don't have to look at Daphne. 'I don't know,' I say quietly.

Five

Daphne gets the boys some ice-cream and they go and eat it in front of the TV. She invites me to join them but I don't really feel like sitting there, watching some kiddie show. I fill in some time warming up milk for Poss and then feeding her with the pipette. Every time I feed her she drinks more, which is good.

After that I decide to take a shower. It'll give me something to do and also save me time in the morning when everyone wants to use the bathroom. The only problem is that all my shower stuff is in Eliza's room.

I stand in the hallway outside her room for a minute, and once I've worked up the courage, I slowly open the door. The room is in darkness and I can vaguely make out a shape on Eliza's bed. She must be asleep. I grope my way over to my bed and somehow manage to put Poss in the pet carrier, glad that I thought to put a hot water bottle in it back at home. Then there's some more feeling around until I find my bathroom stuff and finally I creep back out of the room again.

The Mitchells' bathroom looks like a department store. I've never seen so many bottles of shampoo and conditioner in my life. There are at least five different tubes of half-finished toothpaste, plus a whole shelf of perfumes and body sprays. The shower is over the bathtub, and I'm undressed and about to turn on the water when I notice something resting on the side of the bath. It's a razor – one of those plastic, disposable ones.

I pick the razor up and examine it. I've never actually held one of these before. Dad has a beard so he doesn't have to shave, and Mum would never buy something you're supposed to throw away after one or two uses. There's a plastic thing over the head that slides off easily. Underneath are two blades just a few millimetres apart. They look very sharp. I look down at my legs, which are covered with light brown hairs. The hair isn't really obvious – or at least I never thought it was – until you start looking for it. Then I look back at the razor in my hand. It seems like a crazy thing to do – drag this dangerous-looking thing across your body. Which way are you supposed to drag it, anyway – up or down? I think it's mainly curiosity that makes me try it in the end. I tell myself I'm being an anthropologist again.

First thing I do is double-check that the door is locked. The last thing I want is someone walking in on me. Then I balance one foot on the edge of the bath. I put the razor down near my ankle and very slowly pull it up the front of my leg. I'm not sure how far up I'm supposed to go so I stop just under my knee.

When I inspect my leg I can see a hair-free path. It's like when someone pushes a mower through long grass. It's weird, because I couldn't feel anything happening at all. It didn't pull or hurt or anything like that. There's no blood either, which means I didn't cut myself, I guess. I check the razor. A whole lot of hairs are sticking out between the two blades.

My leg looks dumb with just one hair-free stripe, so I decide to keep going. It's fun, in a weird way – kind of like painting, but in reverse. It gets a little tricky around my ankle but I take those bits extra carefully and it's fine. By the time I've finished one leg, the razor is pretty gunked up with hair so I rinse it off under the tap, making sure I swish all the hairs down the plughole. The second leg is quicker to do because I've got the hang of it by then.

In less than five minutes both my legs are smooth, shiny and hair-free. It's funny how good I feel. Lighter or something. Finally I stand in front of the mirror and lift up my arm. A few strokes and you'd never know there'd been hair there at all.

I hop into the shower. As the water falls over me I run my hands down over my legs. They feel so different – super smooth and sleek. Like they belong to someone else.

After the shower I get into my PJs and head back to Eliza's room. It's still in darkness, which is fine by me. It's only about eight-thirty so it's earlier than I normally go to sleep, but bed feels like the best option. I don't really want to get stuck in the lounge room with Daphne.

The air mattress wobbles and squeaks every time I move. I lie very still, feeling uncomfortable and alone.

I'm just drifting off when I hear a strange noise. It takes me a while to figure out what it is: Eliza is crying. The sound is muffled – like she's doing it under her pillow or the doona.

'Eliza? Are you all right?' Somehow it's easier to talk to her in the dark. To tell her I feel bad about what happened in the kitchen. 'I'm sorry about what I said. I should've kept my mouth shut.'

Okay, so Eliza hasn't exactly been the friendliest person to me, but it's still awful to think that I might be the reason she's crying. Me and my big, fat, truth-telling mouth. The crying suddenly stops but Eliza doesn't reply. Maybe she's fallen asleep. Or maybe she just doesn't want anything to do with me.

I lie there, not sure if I should keep talking or just shut up. The noise finally stops, and after a while I hear Eliza breathing in a way that I know means she's asleep.

But I'm now wide-awake. My eyes have adjusted to the darkness, and when I hear Poss stir in her pet carrier, I take her on my lap to give her some more milk and a pat. Mum has told me a million times that it's not a good idea to treat a wild animal like a pet. You want the animal to stay wild, and being wild means being wary of humans. But I can't help myself. Poor Poss. At least my parents are only away. She has no-one.

V

I wake up very early the next morning, itching. It feels like my legs are on fire and the more I scratch them, the worse they get. Finally I can't stand it any longer and sneak out to the bathroom to see what the problem is.

When I flick on the bathroom light, I nearly die. My legs are totally covered in a red, bumpy rash. I have the kind of skin that gets a mark just from lightly brushing against something, and because I've been scratching at my legs for hours, they are both a mass of lines and welts. It's not a good look.

My first thought is that I've caught something contagious. Chickenpox or measles or something. I'm even a tiny bit glad because surely my parents will have to come home if I'm sick. Then I discover the same red bumps under my arms and the truth finally dawns on me. I'm not sick. This must be a shaving rash.

I feel like an idiot. Like the world is laughing at me for trying to be more like everyone else. A bit more ordinary. Ha ha. As *if*.

I sneak back into bed, being very quiet. The last thing I want is for Eliza to turn on the lights and see my spotty legs. But there's no chance of going back to sleep, either. I lie there, trying to work out how I'm going to keep the rash hidden from everyone. At this time of year we can choose between wearing our winter uniform to school (which has tights) or our summer one (bare legs with socks). Luckily I grabbed both last night when I was packing my bag. Obviously I'll have to wear the winter one now, which will be okay so long as it's not too hot.

When I check my phone again it's 6 a.m. so I get up and quickly put on my winter uniform. I grab the pet carrier and close the door behind me when I leave the room. The whole house is silent.

In the kitchen I feed Poss and then search around for something for myself. At the back of a cupboard I find an unopened packet of oats, so I make some porridge. I'm just putting it into a bowl when someone behind me says, 'What's that?' It's the smaller boy – Oscar – dressed in his PJs with his hair standing up all over the place. He's kind of cute now that he's not trying to kill his brother.

'It's porridge,' I say. 'You know – like the three bears eat. Want to try some?'

Oscar slides into a chair. 'Okay,' he says.

I put a small scoop into a bowl for him and slice up a banana that I've found in the mostly empty fruit bowl. Then I drizzle on a tiny bit of honey and pour on some milk.

Oscar sniffs at it then takes a tiny mouthful. He nods. 'It's good!' he says.

A few minutes later Daphne comes in. She stares at Oscar's bowl in surprise. 'Are you eating *banana*?' she says. Then she looks at me like I've performed some kind of miracle.

'It's not banana,' corrects Oscar. 'It's porridge. Like the three bears eat. And Sophie is Goldilocks.'

Daphne laughs. 'Well, you're officially on breakfast duty, Goldilocks,' she says to me.

I shrug. 'Sure,' I say. I like cooking. At home I never get to make breakfast. My mum is up really early to do her yoga and by the time I get up, breakfast is already laid out and waiting. It's nice to get a chance to do it for once.

When Thomas comes out and sees what Oscar's eating, he wants some too and I end up making more. I don't mind, though. Feels like I'm doing something right around here at last, and it also takes my mind off my itchiness.

It's not until Daphne hands me a bag with my lunch in it and says, 'Okay, gang, it's time to go!' that I realise Eliza hasn't surfaced yet. She finally appears when we're literally walking out the front door. She flicks her hair over her shoulder as she walks past me and I suddenly feel stupid for worrying about making her cry.

I take Poss back to my room. We're not allowed to bring animals to school, but at the last minute I change my mind and hide Poss in her pouch under my jumper. Maybe I'll get in trouble, but it's worth the risk if it means I can keep her safe with me all day.

When I get outside, the Mitchells have all piled into Daphne's huge people mover. The engine is running. Daphne winds down the window. 'Coming with us?'

I shake my head and point to where my bike is leaning. 'No, thanks. I'll ride.'

'Mum,' says Thomas from the back seat. 'Oscar keeps undoing his seatbelt.'

'I don't want a dumb belt!' Oscar yells.

Daphne tries pleading with him, which doesn't work, and for some reason I hear myself saying, 'How about I do it for you, Oscar?' I'm not expecting it to make any difference but, to my astonishment (and probably to everyone else's), Oscar lets me. I get another grateful look from Daphne. I'm fully expecting another glare from Eliza, but she's focused on her phone.

Eventually Daphne drives away and I head off on my bike. I'm starting to think this is going to be the longest week of my life.

Six

Leni is at training before school today and Anya's not here yet. I hate mornings like this, when neither of my best friends are around. It makes me remember what it was like in the first couple of weeks of high school when I didn't really know anyone and spent all the breaks alone or in the library. At least I've got Poss, though, hidden away beneath my jumper.

I'm just feeding Poss some milk on a bench in a quiet spot near the library when Erin comes around the corner. Her face lights up when she sees Poss.

'Oh my god, that is so *cute!*' she says, sitting beside me. 'Where did it come from?' I tell her Poss's story and explain how I'm nursing her just until she's strong enough to fend for herself. 'You poor little thing,' says Erin, leaning in and talking softly to Poss. 'What were you doing at the pool, anyway?'

'They've got some big trees there,' I say. 'And I guess as more and more bushland gets cleared away the animals have to live wherever they can.'

Erin sits up straight and frowns. 'That's terrible!'

'Yeah, I know.'

'I wish I could *do* something,' Erin sighs.

'You could come to the Save the Forest rally,' I say. 'It's in town on Saturday.' To be honest, it's not a serious suggestion so I'm surprised when Erin jumps on it.

'That's a great idea! Are you organising a group from school? Because I'd definitely come.'

'Well, I wasn't really planning to,' I say. The thing is, earlier in the year I did try to get people together for a rally. But hardly anyone showed and I ended up feeling stupid. But Erin won't let the idea go.

'Let's meet at lunchtime,' she says. 'We should make a banner or something like that. So everyone knows where we're from.'

'Just you and me?' I say doubtfully. 'Won't we look a bit dumb?'

'No, we'll tell everyone about it,' says Erin. 'I bet lots of people will be interested in coming.'

I'm not nearly so sure.

Someone's hands wrap around my eyes. 'Guess who?' There's only one person who ever does this.

'Hmm … Anya?' I say.

The hands fly away and Anya bounces in front of me, grinning. She's been a lot happier since her parents finally sold their house. And it's amazing how well she's doing in maths, too. She still refuses to do any maths competitions but Leni and I are both working on her.

'What are you guys talking about?' she asks.

'Soph is organising a group for the forest rally on Saturday,' says Erin. I never actually said I would organise anything, but Erin's still talking. 'You guys will come, won't you?'

Anya shakes her head. 'Not this time. Anyway, Soph can save the forests without my help, can't you, Soph?' Then she raises her arms up in the air like she's making an announcement to a huge crowd. Or like she's a magician. 'Watch while my friend, Sophie Bennett, single-handedly saves the entire planet!'

Erin and I crack up – it's impossible not to when Anya's on a roll – just as Leni arrives, along with Adam and Josh. Leni's friend Jo is with them too. She has her camera slung around her neck as usual.

'What's so funny?' Josh asks.

Erin explains about the rally. 'Can we count you guys in?' she asks.

'I'm already going,' says Jo. 'With my mums.' The first time I heard Jo talk about having two mums, I thought it was really strange. It's funny how normal it seems to me now.

'What about the rest of you?' asks Erin.

'Sure, I'd love to go,' says Josh. And I swear he looks *right at me* as he says it. My 'like' gauge goes berserk.

'What about you, Adam?' says Erin.

Adam shrugs. 'I'm not sure,' he says. 'I've already got

plans on Saturday.' He looks at me curiously. 'Don't you get tired of always organising things and protesting about stuff?' he asks.

Anya wraps her arm around me. 'Are you kidding?' she says. 'Soph *lives* for this kind of thing, don't you, Soph? If she didn't have protests to organise she wouldn't know what else to do with her time.'

'I bet it's more that she knows if she *doesn't* do it, no-one else will,' says Jo. She's right. I can think of lots of things I'd rather do than spend my lunchtimes making banners and handing out flyers.

'Hey,' says Erin suddenly. 'You should do a thing for assembly. Like the one you did when you were trying to change the canteen food.'

A couple of months ago I did this campaign to try to get more ethical and Fairtrade food into the canteen. I don't feel right eating something that comes from factories where they use child labour, or don't pay their workers fairly. And I wanted to get rid of the muesli bars and snacks that had palm oil in them. Orangutans, tigers and rhinos in South-East Asia are dying all the time because their rainforests are being cut down for palm-oil plantations. For me, the stuff just doesn't taste good once I know that.

But a lot of people don't feel the same and I was given a pretty hard time about my canteen campaign. Even my friends thought I'd gone crazy. Whenever I tried to talk about it, no-one wanted to listen. They'd just laugh or roll their eyes. In the end I got so mad that I put together this thing – a presentation – and I showed it at one of our school assemblies. I didn't want to do much talking so instead I found pictures on the internet of the rainforests before and after they'd been destroyed for palm oil. I showed shots of the orangutans whose habitat was disappearing. In the background I had the sound of a forest gradually being replaced by chainsaws and that horrible cracking sound of trees falling, and I showed some of the products that contain palm oil – it's in everything from bread to shampoo.

When I started my presentation, a bunch of idiots started slow-clapping, like it was all just totally boring. Some people even booed – I guess because they were mad I was trying to take away their favourite snacks. I felt so alone and horrible up there on the stage. But I was determined to get through the whole thing, even if everyone booed all the way through it. Because just once, I wanted everyone else to know about the things that worry me. I guess I was hoping there might be one other person who felt a tiny bit the same.

I can't tell you if my presentation made any difference, but at least by the end of it no-one was slow-clapping or booing anymore. It was actually very quiet. Maybe people were listening, maybe they'd nodded off. I didn't really care. I was just glad I got a chance to say it.

The school didn't get rid of all the bad food, but they did start stocking some of the replacement ones I suggested so I guess I achieved *something* – even if I'm the only person who ever buys those things. But honestly? I'm not sure the effort was worth it.

Poss chooses that moment to stick her head out from the edge of my jumper. Everyone laughs in surprise and, quick as a flash, Jo snaps a picture.

'That's a great shot even if I do say so myself!' she pronounces and we all look at it on the display window.

Jo's right. Poss is at her wide-eyed, super-cute best.

'Are you allowed to bring a possum to school?' Leni asks.

'Well, no,' I admit. 'But she's going to stay well hidden, aren't you, Poss? So no-one will know about it.'

The bell goes and as we head off to class, I catch Josh giving me another one of his looks. Does he think it's cool or gross to have a possum hidden under your jacket? I really can't tell.

V

The turnout for our rally meeting at lunchtime is pretty small. No surprises there. It's just me, Erin, George, Leni and Josh. Anya is there, because the rest of us are, but she's still saying she probably won't come on Saturday. Adam's not there but he's told Josh that he might come on Saturday now, and Erin says Phoebe and Jagath will come along, too. We've all brought our lunches with us and we have a sort-of picnic, sharing stuff around. And I can't help noticing that Josh sits right next to me.

We chat about what we want to write on our banner.

George suggests 'Students for trees', but Erin wants 'Teens for trees'. Then Josh says, 'What about "Give trees a chance"?' which I think is cool. Josh is actually pretty funny. People just don't always notice because he gets drowned out by Adam. By the time the bell goes, we still haven't settled on anything but it's been a friendly meeting. I'm feeling happy, especially with Poss sleeping soundly and warmly in her pouch.

I'm halfway to maths class before I realise I've left my textbook in my locker. 'Don't wait,' I tell Leni and Anya. 'I'll catch you up.' There's no point all three of us getting in trouble with Mr Cartwright for being late.

As I turn into the corridor I can see there's something on my locker. It's a note, folded in half and stuck down with tape. Inside is a bit of digital artwork and it sort of reminds me of the graffiti down at the skate park – *Miss Everything* with her big shoes. This is also of a girl in bathers, but she's covered in hair. Her legs are hairy and so are her arms, and there's masses of the stuff curling out from her armpits. She even has a moustache. The hair on her head is long and sticking out everywhere in big, matted dreadlocks. I know straight away that it's meant to be me. Written underneath in big red letters are the words: *Dirty Hippie.*

There are footsteps from around the corner and I shove the note in my pocket just before the principal, Mrs Brinkman, appears. She's surprised to see me. 'Why aren't you in class, Sophie? Is everything okay?'

Poss chooses that moment to become active and her head peers out from around the edge of my blazer.

Mrs Brinkman is silent for a moment. Then she says, 'This is not the right place for a wild animal, Sophie. It can stay for today, but tomorrow it stays at home.'

I nod and mutter, 'Okay, Mrs Brinkman,' and I flee to maths. As I hurry I can hear the note crinkling in my pocket.

Seven

I manage to stop myself from looking at the note during the whole of our maths class (because Mr Cartwright is the kind of teacher who can hear a note rustling from a kilometre away), but I can *feel* it burning a hole in my pocket. I can guess who drew it. Nelson Cooke. I do wonder for a split second if it was Leo Flynn, the guy who I'm pretty sure did *Miss Everything*. But he really doesn't seem like the kind of person who'd do something like this.

In between maths and our next class (science), I go to the bathroom and sneak another look at the note.

On second viewing I can see that the drawing is nowhere as good as Leo's, even though the person has tried to copy his style. So now I'm positive it was Nelson. What I'm not sure of is what to do about it.

V

In science, Mrs Franks gives us a diagram of a dissected rat. We're supposed to label the different organs, then colour them all in with different textas so we can easily identify them. I put my head down and work solidly, glad for the distraction.

When Mrs Franks looks over my shoulder, she laughs. 'That's the most beautifully coloured-in rat I've ever seen, Sophie,' she says. 'Have you changed your mind about doing the actual dissection?'

This is a joke, of course. Our class is dissecting a rat soon and everyone is supposed to participate – no exceptions. But there's no way *I'm* cutting up a rat. I told Mrs Franks this and at first she kept saying, 'You have to do it, Sophie, just like everyone else.' But I kept on about it and she eventually told me to write a two-page essay explaining 'my objections'. I ended up writing *ten* pages. I told her I thought it was wrong that humans did things like that to animals just because we're bigger and smarter. I said it was cruel to kill all those animals just so we could look inside them. I told her I've been a vegetarian my entire life and I never wear leather or fur. I also explained the things we could do to learn the same information without killing an animal. Like, there are these computer programs with 3-D simulations of a rat's internal organs. We could look at those instead. There are lots of educational films that cover this stuff too.

After Mrs Franks read my essay, she said I didn't have to do the dissection. 'I admire your principles,' she said, 'even if I don't agree with you.' She still likes to tease me about it, though. Pretend there's a chance I'll change my mind. No-one knows exactly when the rat day is – she deliberately hasn't said so that people wont be 'sick' that day – but it must be soon.

The colouring helps take my mind off the note. But towards the end of the lesson, the classroom gets really warm and my legs get all itchy again. I can't wait to get home and take my tights off.

V

I cop the usual bike-related abuse on the ride home ('Are you part of a circus?') but it doesn't bother me too much. It's good to be moving, although as I start to sweat, the itchiness gets worse. It feels weird not turning in at our front gate, but I'm so desperate to get out of these tights that I don't think about it much. Daphne opens the front door as I'm dumping my bike around the side of the house.

'We should put that in the back shed,' she says. 'It'd be terrible if it was stolen.'

'I'd be happy if someone stole it,' I say. I guess I'm a little grumpy.

'Really?' says Daphne, surprised. 'But I always thought it was such a *you* bike.'

I shake my head. 'It's not a *me* bike at all. A *me* bike wouldn't have ribbons on it, for a start. It would be shiny green. And it wouldn't weigh 500 kilos.'

Daphne looks like she's about to say something, but then the phone rings and she goes off to answer it. There's no sign of Eliza, which is good, because it means I can quickly get changed in her room.

I peel off my tights and give my legs a good scratch. The welts reappear instantly. Seriously, if my skin was a person it would be the type that bursts into tears whenever someone gives them a funny look. I go through my bag for something else to put on and realise with a lurch that I've left my jeans at home. All I have is the skirt I was wearing yesterday and some shorts, neither of which will cover my legs. Even worse – I don't have my door key so I can't go and let myself in. Daphne probably has a spare but she'll want to know what I need it for. In the end, there's nothing for it but to pull on the tights again.

I transfer Poss into the pet carrier and head outside. I'll do my homework out there, I decide. The breeze might help with the itching.

The two boys are in the yard, whacking their one stunted tree with a stick.

'What are you doing?' I say.

'We're bored,' grumbles Oscar. 'The Wii broke.'

There's no way I can do my homework or feed Poss while they're doing this. I'll have to distract them.

'Well, how about you pretend you're inside a Wii game?' I suggest. I don't know anything about Wii and I'm fully expecting the boys to say it's a dumb idea, but they both jump up straight away, looking excited.

'Yeah!' they say. 'Let's pretend we're inside Super Galaxy Adventure.'

'Hey, not me!' I say. 'I've got homework. And anyway, I don't know how to play it.' But the boys keep begging and in the end I can see it's going to be easier – and quicker – just to join in for a while.

It turns into a crazy game – partly because I know nothing about Super Galaxy Adventure and partly because the boys keep changing the rules, but they're happy just to have me chasing them around. I have to keep changing into things – like a boulder that's trying to roll over them or a giant bird that wants to catch them in its beak. Soon I'm totally exhausted, but I'm laughing a lot too. They're growing on me, I guess, these boys.

'I'm just going to the toilet,' I call as I escape inside. The running around has made me really hot and my legs are burning. I rush to the bathroom and push down my tights so I can give my legs a good scratch. They look like a total mess.

I'm mid-scratch when the door flings back and Eliza walks in. Her eyes go huge with shock when she sees my legs and her mouth falls open. 'What's wrong with your legs?' she asks.

If I was a different person – Anya, for instance – I might have told her that I have some rare, contagious disease and that she should stay away from me. But I'm not Anya. So I tell her the truth.

'I shaved them yesterday and I got a rash.'

Eliza keeps staring at my legs, her forehead creased. 'Does that *usually* happen when you shave?' she asks.

'I don't know,' I admit. 'I've never shaved before.'

'You must have really sensitive skin,' says Eliza.

'Yep,' I say. 'Super-sensitive.'

'What shaving cream did you use? Or did you just make a lather with soap?'

I shake my head. 'Neither. I just shaved them dry.'

Eliza gives me a *der* look. 'Well, no wonder you got a rash,' she says. 'You're supposed to wet your skin first, and then use soap or a foam or cream. They've got some good ones at the chemist shop at Westland Mall.'

'Oh,' I say, feeling stupid. Now I think about it, it's obvious that you shouldn't just start scraping a razor against your skin, especially if you've got *emo* skin like mine. I expect Eliza will leap on this chance to laugh at me. But to my surprise, she sits down on the edge of the bath.

'Hey, don't worry about it,' she says. 'Everyone makes mistakes. Look at the mistake I made deciding to go out with Creep Features.'

'Creep Features?' I repeat. 'Do you mean … *Nelson*?'

Eliza smiles – a kind of sad, tired smile. 'That's my new name for him. Do you like it?'

'I love it,' I say. 'It fits him perfectly.'

For a moment I consider telling Eliza about the note. Even showing it to her. But I chicken out. Eliza is being friendly right now, but who knows how long that will last – or if it's even for real?

'So does that mean you guys aren't going out anymore?' I ask.

Eliza nods and slumps down onto the side of the tub. 'I dumped him today. In front of all his soccer friends.'

I find myself grabbing Eliza's hand and shaking it. 'Good one,' I say.

Eliza's smile looks a little happier. 'Thanks.'

I feel like I need to apologise to her again, just in case she didn't hear me last night. 'I'm really sorry about how I told you. About Nelson cheating on you, I mean. It can't have been the best way to find out.'

Eliza raises her shoulders and lets them fall slowly. 'Well, at least you were honest about it,' she says. 'After I dumped him, some of my friends admitted they knew he was cheating on me, but they didn't say anything because they were afraid of upsetting me.' She gives a short snorty laugh. 'I guess they were trying to be nice, but I've been thinking about it all day and I've decided that I'd rather know the truth.'

'Even if it hurts?' I say.

Eliza thinks about this. 'Yeah, I think so.'

'Me too,' I say. 'It's always better to know.'

'You've got to stop doing that,' says Eliza and I realise that I've started scratching my legs again.

'I *can't*,' I groan.

Eliza gets up and opens the bathroom cupboard, moves a few things around, then extracts a bottle. 'This stuff should help,' she says, handing it to me. 'We used it when Thomas had chickenpox and couldn't stop scratching.'

The stuff in the bottle is sort of pink and milky-looking. It smells weird but right now I would happily rub my legs with fish guts if I thought it would help.

'I'm such a moron,' I say, looking down at my poor legs as I dab the lotion on with cotton wool. It's soothing, but my legs are now pretty gunky. Eliza suddenly grins at me, which takes me by surprise.

'Hey, if it makes you feel any better, I shaved off an entire eyebrow once,' says Eliza.

'No way!' I say, laughing. 'Really?'

'Yeah, it was before we moved here,' Eliza explains. 'I decided my eyebrows were too bushy so I tried to shape them with a razor.'

'So is that why you guys moved here?' I ask jokily. 'Because the whole missing-eyebrow thing made it too embarrassing to stay where you were?'

The smile instantly disappears from Eliza's face. 'No, that's not why we moved,' she says quietly. 'We moved because my dad died and we had to sell our old house. He had cancer.'

There's not much you can say after you've put your foot in it that badly – just *I'm sorry.* Which is what I say. Then I add. 'I didn't know.'

'Really?' says Eliza, picking at a hole in the hem of her jumper. 'I thought everyone knew. I thought everyone was whispering about it behind my back. That's what it felt like, at least when we first moved here.' The hole in Eliza's jumper is growing. 'Which is why it always drives me crazy when Mum goes on her whole *let's focus on the positive* thing. Like, how can anything be positive after your dad has died?'

It's strange how finding out something like this can change everything. My image of Eliza is completely different now. It's like one of those colour-by-numbers pictures where, just by adding one colour, the picture suddenly morphs from a bunch of random blotches into something you can recognise. A picture you understand.

'Dinner!' calls Daphne down the hallway. 'Come and get it while it's hot!'

'Wait there for a mo,' says Eliza to me and dashes out. She's back in a minute with a pair of tracksuit pants. 'Wear these until that rash calms down a bit.'

At dinner (pasta and tomato sauce), Daphne makes us play the 'best thing' game again. The boys say that the best thing was playing 'pretend Wii' with me.

'Yeah,' I say. 'That was my highlight too.' I'm glad we're not listing our worst things. The sooner I forget about that horrible note, the better.

Eliza says her best thing was 'Being a single woman again', and gives me a smile.

Everyone helps to clear away dinner and the boys go and turn on the TV.

'I guess I'll go and have a shower,' I say as I put the last bits away.

'Why don't you come and watch tellie with us?' suggests Daphne.

'Yeah, come on,' says Eliza.

'Well, okay,' I say. 'Sure.'

The show the boys are watching is pretty dumb, but they both think it's hilarious and crack up over every tiny thing. That makes the rest of us laugh. Then Daphne starts tickling them, making them laugh even more.

'Mum,' says Eliza, rolling her eyes. 'That's not the way to tickle them. You have to do it like this.' She waggles her hands in the air for a moment, then launches herself at the boys. They shriek with delight.

It's noisy and I get kicked (accidentally) in the stomach a few times, but it's nice too. As I head off to shower I feel a bit guilty that I've wasted an hour doing nothing except watching TV – but then maybe that's okay. Maybe wasting time is sometimes the best thing you *can* do.

In the shower, I wash off the lotion and I'm relieved to see that my legs are way less blotchy than before. Hopefully tomorrow I'll be able to wear my summer uniform.

I feed Poss and explain that I can't take her to school in the morning. She doesn't seem too worried. It's not until I'm lying in bed that I realise I hardly thought about the note since I got home. And by then, I'm too tired to think about it anyway.

Eight

The day passes without any major dramas. Poss is a little stronger and much greedier. Daphne agrees to feed her while I'm at school. My rash has pretty much gone. At breakfast Eliza says hi and smiles at me, which I guess means she doesn't regret opening up to me last night. I'm actually feeling a lot more settled at Daphne's place than I thought I would.

The only bad thing is the Nelson stuff. I find a ball of nerves forming in my stomach as I walk towards my locker, wondering if there will be another note there. My biggest fear is that if there is one, someone else will read it first. That would be awful. It's not so bad when it's only me who knows about it. I figure I can ignore it. But if my friends found out it would become a 'thing'. Luckily, the day passes without a note appearing.

It's a busy day. School is really full-on, plus we have another meeting at lunchtime to discuss the rally. We still can't agree on what we should write on the banner, so we put it off until Friday because that's the only time we're all free. It has to be done then, no matter what. And when I get home from school there's Poss to take care of, plus Oscar and Thomas are waiting to drag me off to play with them, even though the Wii is fixed now.

At breakfast on Wednesday morning, Eliza completely surprises me by asking if I want to go to Westland Mall that afternoon.

'I need to get some stuff from the chemist shop,' she says, giving me a meaningful look. 'Wasn't there some stuff you needed, too?' I know she's talking about the shaving cream for sensitive skin. I haven't really decided if I'm going to try shaving again. But I guess it wouldn't hurt to be prepared just in case there is a next time.

'All right. Thanks, I'll come,' I say.

Eliza looks over at her mum. 'Is that okay, Mum?'

'Sounds like a great idea,' says Daphne, and I can see that she's really happy Eliza and I are getting along. 'You'd better get a lift in the car this morning, though, Sophie,' Daphne points out. 'You won't be able to take your bike on the bus to the mall.'

Even though the car is massive, it feels pretty squishy in there with all our bags and stuff. It's bumpy in the back too, and I have to wind the window down so I don't get sick. Much as I dislike my ugly bike, I have to say that cycling is a much nicer way to travel than being in the car.

I wasn't planning on telling my friends about the Westland Mall trip, but Anya invites us to her mum's place after school and I tell them why I can't go. Anya and Leni stare in surprise when I tell them I'm going shopping with Eliza.

'You're friends now?' says Anya. 'I thought you couldn't stand her.'

'Yeah,' says Leni. 'I thought you said you had nothing in common.'

'We don't, really,' I say. 'But it's different when you live with someone for a while. You – I guess you find out more about what they're really like.' I don't want to explain about Eliza's dad, or about the shaving stuff, so I leave it there.

Leni tilts her head. 'I thought you weren't allowed to go to the mall on your own?'

This is true. My parents aren't fans of the mall anyway and they definitely wouldn't let me go on my own. I wonder for a moment if I'm doing the wrong thing. If I shouldn't go. But as I'm thinking it, I realise how much I really *do* want to go.

'My parents aren't here,' I say, shrugging. After that I change the topic.

To be honest, I'm half-expecting Eliza to change her mind about going to the mall with me. But when I walk out of our classroom that afternoon, there she is, waiting for me.

'Ready to go?' she says. 'The bus goes from round the corner.'

Generally when I go to the mall (which isn't very often) it's with my parents, who basically want to get in and out of there as quickly as possible. They spend the whole time complaining about how awful everything is. The music. The crowds. The smell of the food court. The lack of windows. It's very different being there with someone who isn't in a desperate hurry to get out again.

We head up to the second floor and walk past the Sport Smart store to a huge chemist shop. Eliza leads me expertly through the aisles until we stop in front of the shaving stuff. There are lots of packets of razors – disposable blue ones for men and pink ones for women, as well as cans of shaving cream and tubes of stuff for people with sensitive skin. Eliza selects a packet of pink disposable razors.

'These have a strip of aloe vera on the top which is good for people with skin like yours,' she says.

'You mean weird, blotchy, rashy skin?' I say, grinning at her.

Eliza smiles back. 'Hey, you've got nice skin,' she tells me. 'You just have to accept it for what it is. And treat it properly.'

Eliza searches through the creams and lotions and pulls out one that's good for people with *extra-sensitive skin*. 'This is what you need,' she says, handing it to me. 'And a good moisturiser like this one to put on afterwards.'

I hold the bottles in my hands. They feel cool and smooth and foreign. 'I'm not sure about this . . .' I say.

I can see annoyance flickering on Eliza's face. 'Why? Do you *want* to keep getting rashes?'

'Well, no,' I say. I hesitate and then decide to explain what's holding me back. Even if it makes her think I'm some weirdo hippie. 'It's just that this has probably all been tested on animals. They stick it in their eyes and stuff to see if it's going to cause people any problems. It's cruel.'

The moisturiser my mum uses comes from the co-op shop where she volunteers on Saturdays. When she runs out she takes the jar back to refill it. We get our washing-up liquid, our soap and shampoo from the same place. None of it is tested on animals.

Eliza looks at me strangely, but doesn't say anything. Instead, she takes the bottles from my hands and returns them to the shelf. When she starts walking away, I figure she's given up on me. But then she turns around and says, 'Come on,' beckoning for me to follow.

We go right to the back of the store where there is a small range of cruelty-free products. Unlike in the other section, where there were heaps of sensitive shaving creams to choose from, here there's only one and it's more expensive than any of the others. But I feel way better about it, knowing that it didn't get stuck in some poor rabbit's eyes.

Eliza examines the rest of the stuff with interest. 'Look, there's even make-up,' she says, holding up an eyeliner.

I laugh and shake my head. 'No thanks,' I say. 'That's really not me.'

Eliza gives me this look then, and says, 'Not really *you*? Or not really your mum?'

I don't know what to say to that. I guess there are a lot

of things I would say about myself that are also about my mum. *We* don't eat meat. *We* don't like cars. *We* think it's cruel to experiment on animals. *We* don't wear make-up. I've never thought about whether those things were really, genuinely *me* or not.

Eliza waves her hand in front of my face. 'You've gone all dreamy!' she laughs. 'Come on. Let's go buy this stuff.'

As we're heading for the checkout, we run into one of Eliza's friends – Lara.

'What are you doing here?' she asks. She says it to Eliza but I get the feeling that what she really means is, 'What are you doing here with *her?*'

'We're just shopping,' says Eliza.

'Want to come to the food court?' says Lara. 'I'm meeting some of the others there. But not Nelson, don't worry.'

I'm expecting Eliza to say a quick 'See you later!' to me and head off with her friend. But instead, she turns to me. 'Want to go?' she says.

I'm not sure what to say. It's nice of her to invite me, but on the other hand it's not really me, hanging out at the food court with Eliza and her friends. But even as I think this – *not really me* – I start to wonder. I mean, I've never done it, so how can I possibly know if it's *me* or not? So I nod.

'Yeah, sure. I'll come. Thanks.'

V

The moment we arrive in the food court, though, I instantly feel like I've made a huge mistake. Eliza's friends are crowded around a big table, laughing and joking together. Hazel and Edi are there too, with Archie de Souza and Leo Flynn. My stomach curls. I'm ninety per cent sure that Leo didn't draw that awful picture of me, but maybe he's seen it. Maybe they've *all* seen it and are laughing at me.

'Uh, maybe I'll just go,' I mutter to Eliza. But she doesn't hear me. Or maybe she chooses not to.

'Save me a spot,' she says. 'I'll go and get us something to eat.' She heads off to one of the food counters.

I stand there feeling like a total idiot. No-one seems to even notice I'm there. Then someone calls me.

'Soph!'

The voice seems to be floating above me. I look up. It's Josh, coming down the escalators with a Sport Smart bag in his hand. He's grinning like he hasn't seen me for years, rather than just a couple of hours. But I'm grinning back because I'm really, really pleased to see his friendly face.

'What are *you* doing here?' he says as he gets off the escalator.

'I'm shopping with Eliza,' I say, like this is the most normal thing in the world. 'We've just stopped for something to eat.'

'Great idea,' says Josh. 'Mind if I sit down?'

Of course, I don't mind at all and Josh tells the others to shove over so there's room for us. I end up squeezed next to Leo. He smiles at me. 'You're Sophie, right?' he says.

I nod.

'You know, there's something I've always wanted to tell you,' he says.

My heart beats at double-speed. *He's* got something he wants to say to *me?*

'I haven't touched anything with palm oil in it since

you did that thing at assembly. My mum thinks I'm nuts because I'm always checking the labels of the stuff she buys.'

Hazel leans over. 'Oh yeah, that presentation was so horrible. I had nightmares for weeks with all these sad orangutans in it. I got up one night and signed this online petition so I could finally go to sleep.'

'Wow,' I say, which I know is totally lame but I am completely shocked. I had no idea anyone was listening that day. I definitely didn't realise it had an effect on anyone.

Eliza comes back and we all shuffle around a bit more. She hands me a drink and a wrap. She's got one for herself too. I'm not actually hungry but I take a bite. And then I stop with my mouth full because there's this really strong flavour in the wrap. One I don't recognise. The texture is really strange too. Eliza sees my expression, looks down at her own wrap, then at mine, her eyes wide.

'Stop!' she barks. 'I gave you the wrong one. That one's got salami in it.'

Everyone goes quiet. I guess they're waiting to see how

I'll react. Freak? Spit the food out? The thing is, I'm not really sure *how* to react. I've never eaten meat before.

But in the end I just swallow the food in my mouth.

Eliza laughs. 'I wasn't expecting you to do that!' she says. 'Good for you!'

'I wasn't expecting it either,' says Josh. But he doesn't add *good for you*.

I do feel good, though. Or at least different. It feels great to do something unpredictable. That's probably why I take another bite, then another and another, until the entire wrap is completely gone.

V

Eliza and I catch the bus back to her place and although we don't talk much, it feels like a good silence. The sort you can have when you're friends with someone. My shaving cream and moisturiser are tucked away in my schoolbag and I'm feeling pretty good as we turn into the Mitchells' driveway.

The door opens and Daphne appears. She has a strange

expression on her face. 'I'm so sorry, Sophie,' she says. 'I have some bad news.'

My insides lurch. At first I think it's my parents, that something's happened to them. Then I'm equally sure that it's Poss. I never should've left her here by herself all day.

'Your bike is missing,' says Daphne. 'Soph, I'm so sorry – I think it's been stolen.'

'No way,' I say. 'Someone stole *my* bike?' It's such a strange, crazy thing to hear that I don't know whether to laugh or cry.

Nine

Having no bike means that I have to get a lift in the morning with Daphne, so I'm already feeling a little queasy when I walk into our science classroom and a terrible stink hits me in the face.

'Pee-yew!' says Anya, holding her nose. 'What happened in here, Mrs Franks? Did something die in here overnight?'

Mrs Franks smiles. 'Not quite,' she says.

Leni suddenly stops in her tracks and starts poking me in the side with her finger.

'What?' I say.

She points to the front bench. Lined up across it are some smallish white boards. And pinned to these are rats. I freeze, not wanting to look but also unable *not* to look.

Other people arrive.

'Hey, is it cut-up-a-rat day today?' says one of the boys, pushing past me. 'Cool!'

Leni looks at me with a worried face. 'Are you okay?' she whispers.

'Yeah, I'm fine,' I say automatically. Even though I'm not really sure that I am. Part of me just wants to get out of there as quickly as possible, but I'm feeling a little wobbly so I decide the best thing to do right now is sit down.

I slide into my seat just as Mrs Franks starts giving everyone the rules for the dissection. There's a sheet for us to follow, telling us where to cut and which tools to use to do it.

'Cutting through the rib cage can take a little more effort than you think,' she tells us. There's another sheet for us to mark off the rat's internal organs as we see them. The whole thing seems surreal to me, but there are a few people actually laughing. Suddenly Mrs Franks put her hands on the table and looks around at us.

'This is not a time for joking around,' she warns us. 'These animals have given up their lives so that you can learn more about how bodies work.' *Given up their lives.* She makes it sound like the animals chose this fate – which of course they didn't. Normally I'd point this out to Mrs Franks, but at the moment I'm having trouble getting any words out.

'If I see anyone messing around with the specimens, they will not only fail this semester but they will be suspended. This is school policy,' she adds, 'so don't make the mistake of thinking it's just a hollow threat on my part.'

Everyone quietens down after that and Mrs Franks starts going through the different tools we will need. The scalpel. The surgical scissors. The tiny tweezers.

'Right,' she says eventually. 'Time to start. Pair up, everybody. I'll come around and hand out the specimens.' Then she turns to me. 'Sophie, I've got some worksheets for you to do. Do you want to take them to the library?'

Words come out of my mouth. Words that hardly feel

connected to me but I know I'm saying them. 'Actually, I think I'll stay,' I say. 'I'll just watch the dissection. If that's okay.'

Everyone stares at me like I've gone mad. Maybe I have. But I guess I've been thinking a lot about what Eliza said. About why I do stuff, or don't do stuff. Is it because of what my parents believe in, or because of what *I* believe in? It seems important to start working this out.

I know I feel bad about all these rats dying just so we can cut them up. *Really* bad. But what if one person in the class ends up becoming a doctor or a scientist because of what they learn today? What if they then go on and discover a cure for some horrible disease, like the kind of cancer that killed Eliza's dad? What if *my* dad got sick? Wouldn't I want someone to find a cure – even if it meant that rats had to die? The more I think about it, the more confused I get.

'Of course it's okay, Sophie,' says Mrs Franks, once she's recovered from her surprise. 'You can watch Anya and Leni.'

The moment Mrs Franks moves away, Leni hisses,

'What are you doing, Soph? I thought you were totally against this.' My friends are both looking a little freaked out. It's like I'm suddenly not the person they thought I was. Like I'm suddenly not *me*. But there isn't time right now to explain why I've changed my mind. And to be honest, I'm not completely sure I know the reasons myself, other than I suddenly feel like trying things I never thought I would, because I want to see how it feels.

'Are you *sure* about this, Soph?' says Anya. 'I mean, if I had a chance not to do the dissection, I'd take it.'

'Yes, I'm sure,' I say, hoping that by saying it, it'll somehow become true.

Mrs Franks brings our rat over and puts it on the table. I'm in the middle so it goes right in front of me. It's lying on its back with its legs splayed and its head tilted up. It looks like it's asleep, except that there are silver pins in its paws. Mrs Franks gives us some tools and Leni arranges them in front of us. She shakes her head. 'I can't believe we're actually going to do this,' she says.

The classroom has gone quiet – even the guys who were joking around before are suddenly very still. It's like everyone is thinking what Leni just said.

Mrs Franks flicks on the board at the front of the class and a diagram of a rat comes up, with a red dotted line down its chest. 'We'll start off together,' she tells us. 'One person from each group, please take the scalpel.'

Leni and Anya look at each other.

'So,' says Anya, 'who's going to do it?'

I hear myself say, 'I'll do it.' I think I'm just as surprised as Leni and Anya.

I pick up the scalpel. It's about as thick as a pencil, but very smooth and cold and it gleams when the ceiling light catches in its surface.

'Now, place the scalpel here,' says Mrs Franks, pointing to where the dotted line on her rat diagram begins, 'and cut up to here. We'll be cutting through the skin and a layer of fat.'

I position the scalpel over the rat. But then this weird feeling comes over me. It's almost like I'm floating above myself. I can see my friends and the rat on the bench but they seem really far away. Then everything goes kind of grey, like the colour has been turned down on the world.

'I've got to go,' I mutter, dropping the scalpel and running for the door. There's no way I want to faint in the middle of class. All I can hear is a buzzing, ringing noise in my ears.

The corridor outside is quiet and cool. I lean against the wall and take some deep breaths. Slowly the buzzing noise stops and the colour returns.

Mrs Franks comes out and closes the door behind her. 'Are you okay, Sophie?' she says. She doesn't sound cross at me for running out, just concerned.

'I'm fine,' I say. 'I think maybe I'm coming down with something.'

'Maybe,' she agrees, but I can tell she doesn't really think so. 'How about you go for a little walk? Get some air. See how you feel.'

I nod, but don't answer. Mrs Franks pats my shoulder.

'I'm proud of you for giving the dissection a go, Sophie,' she says. 'I know it was hard for you.'

'Thanks,' I mutter, but I don't think there's much to be proud of. No-one else almost passed out before the dissection even properly began.

Mrs Franks goes back into the classroom and I wander off down the corridor, not really knowing where to go. I'm feeling much better now that I'm out of there, with its horrible stink, but I still feel pretty confused. I wish my mum or dad were around so I could talk to them about what happened. But they are far away, and out of mobile phone range. Without meaning to, I end up at the lockers. I spot someone else there. It's Josh. He looks a little pale.

'Hi, Sophie,' he says.

'Hi,' I say, trying to sound light and jokey. 'Shouldn't you be in class, carving up rats? Or were you sent to make sure I haven't crumpled up in a heap somewhere?'

Josh laughs and then suddenly looks embarrassed. 'I couldn't do it,' he admits. 'It just felt really wrong. Cutting up some animal just because I can.'

It's surprising to hear him say this. 'But you eat meat,' I point out. 'That's not so different.'

'I know,' says Josh. 'The thing is …' He gets a funny look on his face. 'Well, I've been thinking about going vego. Or at least, part-time vego.'

'No way!' I say and start laughing.

Josh looks at me. 'What's so funny?'

'Sorry,' I say. 'It's just weird to think that you might go vegetarian in the same week that I eat meat for the first time.'

Josh smiles too. 'True,' he says. 'I was pretty spun out when you ate that salami yesterday. But I get why you did it. It was a test – right? Because that's basically what I'm thinking about this vego idea. I just want to see what it's like.'

Then something weird happens. Josh reaches over my shoulder and for a moment I think he's going to hug me. But instead he pulls off something that's been stuck to the lockers. To *my* locker.

'There's a note for you,' he says. As he hands it to me, it opens up so we can both see the contents. This time there's no picture. Just words.

Question: How do you spell ugly, stinking loser?
Answer: S.O.P.H.I.E B.E.N.N.E.T.T

'Whoa,' says Josh, taking a step back like he's been smacked in the face. 'Who wrote that?'

'No-one,' I say, crumpling it up.

'Sophie,' says Josh, his voice low and serious. 'Have you got notes like this before?'

'One other time,' I admit. 'But seriously, it's no big deal. It doesn't bother me.'

'It bothers *me*,' says Josh flatly. 'You have to tell someone about it. People can't get away with writing stuff like that.'

I shake my head. I don't want everyone to know. In fact, I don't want *anyone* to know. It's too humiliating. 'It's really nice of you to be worried,' I add quickly. 'But I just want to forget it. Anyway, I don't know for sure who did it and I can't go around accusing people.'

Josh keeps insisting that we go straight to Mrs Brinkman and show her the note. And the thing is, while I'm partly terrified he'll do this, I'm also flattered that he's so worked up about it. The gauge in my head has swung right over to 'He likes you'. It's weird to be in the middle of something so horrible, yet still feel this small, good thing happening at the same time.

Finally I get Josh to promise not to say anything to anyone. Not even to Adam.

'But if another note comes, we're going to Mrs Brinkman, okay?' he says.

I agree to this, although I don't really mean it. I'll just have to make sure that if another note *does* appear, I'm the first – and only – person to see it.

Ten

I'm hanging out with Leni at lunchtime when Erin comes up to us. 'I think we should say something about the rally at the school assembly tomorrow,' Erin says. 'A presentation – like the one you did for your canteen campaign. That was amazing.'

I'm starting to realise that more people were paying attention when I did that presentation than I'd thought. But all the same, I shake my head.

'We don't have time,' I say. 'The canteen presentation took ages to put together and I got a lot of help from Leni.'

'I'll help you again,' says Leni. 'In fact, I've got that photo Jo took of your possum on a flash drive. We could start with that. Because that's kind of what this rally is about, isn't it? Making sure there are places for animals like Poss to live?'

'Exactly!' says Erin. Then she gives me a pleading look. 'It doesn't need to be super complex or anything. Just a few pictures to grab everyone's attention while we remind them about the rally.'

In the end I say okay and we head off to the computer lab – me, Erin, Leni and Anya. There's no-one else in the lab when we get there, which is lucky because only a couple of the machines are any good to work on. Leni sits down in front of one and plugs in her flash drive, then opens up a jpeg file. Poss's cute, big-eyed face fills the screen and all of us go *Aww!* at the same time. It's basically impossible not to.

We drop the picture into a Powerpoint document and are deciding what else to put in when Leni looks at the time. 'The bell is about to go,' she says. 'We'd better pack up.' She saves the project and ejects the flash drive.

'Hey, Leni,' says Erin. 'Is that yours too?' She points to a flash drive in the computer next to us.

'No,' says Leni. 'But pass it over. Maybe we can work out whose it is.'

It turns out that the drive itself isn't named, but there are files on it.

'There's one folder called *school stuff* and one called *other stuff*,' Leni reports.

'Have a look in *other stuff*,' suggests Anya.

Leni goes in and then double-clicks randomly on one of the files. It's called *List*.

A document opens on the screen. One we all recognise straight away. *The hot list*. There's complete silence as we stare at it, remembering how we all felt when this list was pinned to our noticeboard a few months ago.

'Do you think this is the actual list?' says Leni.

'It looks the same,' says Anya. 'Edi is at number one and I'm at number twenty.'

'Someone might have just copied it down,' Erin points out. 'You know, because it was *so good* they wanted to remember it.'

That seems pretty unlikely. What's much more likely – and what we all suspect – is that this flash drive belongs to the person who wrote that list.

'How cool would it be if we could prove who created that stupid thing!' says Erin. 'Then we could tell them what we thought of them.'

My heart starts to beat in double-time. I've always suspected Nelson wrote the list. Which makes me nervous about what *else* might be on that drive.

'What about that one?' says Anya, pointing to a file called *note*. 'Maybe it's a letter with a name on it.'

'Is this a good idea?' I say. 'It's sort of like spying, isn't it?'

But the others are so focused on the computer that they don't seem to hear me. My hands start to sweat as the file opens up. It's the first note that was stuck to my locker. The one with the picture of the hairy girl in bathers, with 'dirty hippie' written underneath.

Leni frowns. 'It looks like it's meant to be someone, right?'

Anya nods. 'Yes. But who?'

'It's probably just someone mucking around,' I say, trying to keep the wobble out of my voice. 'A dumb joke. Let's just delete it.'

The others look at me like I've gone mad. 'No way!' says Erin. 'I want to know who owns this drive. That list is horrible – and I think this note is obviously meant to be nasty too. What if it was sent to someone – can you imagine how terrible they would feel?'

Actually, yeah, I *can* imagine. But I can also imagine how ashamed I'm going to feel if they all see the second note – the one that spells out my name. I can already see the file in the list – *SB*.

'Open that one,' says Anya, pointing to a file called *letter*.

Dear Eliza,

I've finally worked out why you would dump me. Here are the reasons:

You are dumb

You are a bitch . . .

The list goes on and on, getting nastier with every point. We read it together in total silence.

'Soph,' says Anya when we're finished. 'Do you know if Eliza broke up with someone recently?'

I nod. 'Nelson,' I say. No-one looks one bit surprised to hear it.

'The trouble is,' says Erin slowly, 'that none of this stuff has his name on it. We need something that links this drive to him.'

'Well, let's keep looking,' says Leni. The next file she opens is *SB*.

Question: how do you spell ugly, stinking loser?

Answer: S.O.P.H.I.E B.E.N.N.E.T.T

Everyone turns to me, and I can tell they're all trying to find something to say.

'Sophie,' says Erin after a minute. 'Have you already seen this?'

I try to laugh but it comes out more like a snort. 'Actually, yes. Today. It was stuck on my locker. And the other one was there a couple of days ago.'

'Oh, Soph,' says Anya, flinging her arms around me. 'Why didn't you tell us?'

'Because it's not a big deal,' I mutter.

Leni puts an arm around me too. 'Of course it's a big deal,' she says softly. 'It's horrible. I'd be devastated if someone sent that to me.'

'It's disgusting,' says Erin, looking angry. 'And really cowardly.'

'So, what are we going to do about it?' asks Leni.

'Take it to Mrs Brinkman, of course,' says Erin promptly. 'Nelson will probably be suspended for this.'

'He should be expelled!' declares Leni, her arm still tight around me. 'He's such a creep.'

Anya looks at me. 'Soph?' she says. 'What do *you* want to do?'

It's a hard question to answer. Part of me just wants to destroy the flash drive and forget all about it. I don't want a whole lot of people reading those notes. It'll be so humiliating. But the thing is, it isn't only about me. There's the hot list. And there's that letter to Eliza. And then there's all the things he hasn't written yet. Other notes. Other letters. If I don't stand up to him, Nelson will keep doing stuff like this, getting stronger and nastier.

Finally I nod.

'Okay,' I say. 'Let's take it to Mrs Brinkman. But we'd better do it now, before I change my mind.'

V

When I get back to the Mitchells' place that afternoon (on the bus, of course, because my bike is still missing), the kitchen door is shut. There's a lot of clanging and talking coming from the other side. I knock.

'Hey, what's going on in there? Can I come in?'

'No!' three voices call out together. It's Daphne and the boys.

'We're cooking a surprise dinner,' Daphne explains. 'You'll have to wait.'

It feels strange being on my own. Eliza's not around either. It's funny how quickly you can get used to something. A few days ago I was dying for some peace and quiet, but now I've got it, I feel – well – a little left out, I guess.

I feed Poss, do my homework and wait for dinner to be ready. Whatever they're doing, it seems to be taking forever.

Finally Oscar and Thomas come and drag me to the table, and they make me sit right at the head while they rush to finish things off in the kitchen. Eliza turns up and goes to help too, and I feel pretty silly sitting there all alone. But the boys look so proud when they carry in the food that my feeling of silliness disappears. They've cooked lasagne – or two lasagnes, to be exact. A meat one and a vegie one.

'It was the boys' idea,' explains Daphne. 'They wanted to make something special because you'll be going home soon and it's been so great having you here.'

'Oh, guys … thanks!' I say. I'm actually feeling a little choked up. 'I've really loved being here. It's been fun.'

To everyone's surprise, Oscar suddenly bursts into loud, messy tears. 'I don't want her to go!' he says, scrambling onto my lap.

'Hey, I'm not going far,' I point out, laughing. 'Just to the other side of the fence.'

'But you're different when you're over there,' Oscar says. 'I like you better when you're here.'

'Well, how about I try to be more like the person I am *here* when I'm back *there*?' I say.

Oscar nods – as though what I've just said makes perfect sense. 'Okay,' he says. 'But you have to promise.'

I cross my heart and promise him and he goes back to his own seat, happy again.

When Daphne offers me the lasagne, I take a small piece of the meat one as well as the vegetarian.

Eliza looks at me curiously. 'Have you given up being vegetarian now?' she asks.

'No,' I say. 'At least, I'm not sure. I guess I want to make sure I'm a vegetarian because I *mean* it, not just because I've always been one.'

Eliza nods. 'That makes sense.' Then she holds her plate out to her mum. 'Can I try the vegetarian one, please?'

V

After dinner we play with the Wii and I surprise everyone (including myself) by being a star at archery.

'It totally fits with you,' laughs Eliza. 'I can just imagine you riding around on horseback in the olden days, firing arrows at the bad guys.'

Later, when we're getting ready for bed, Eliza says something that catches me by surprise. 'Mrs Brinkman called me into her office after school,' she says, really casually. 'She showed me the flash drive and the letter that was written to me.'

'She *showed* you?' I say, shocked. I suppose I thought Eliza wouldn't have to find out about the letter.

Eliza nods. 'She wanted me to say if I knew anyone who would write something like that to me. And of course I did.' She doesn't need to say the name. We both know it.

I climb into my squeaky bed. 'Is it enough proof?' I ask. 'Does she believe it was really Nelson who did all that?'

Eliza nods again. 'He was still at school – at soccer training – so Mrs Brinkman called him into her office too. When she showed him the flash drive he admitted it was his, and all the stuff on it.'

'So what will happen?' I ask.

Eliza shrugs. 'I'm not sure. I think they'll suspend him, but I wouldn't be surprised if he leaves the school anyway. Imagine staying once it gets around what he did.' We're both quiet for a moment, thinking about that.

'You know, you should have told me he wrote those notes to you,' says Eliza. 'Man, he's such a loser.'

It's hard to explain why I didn't tell anyone about the note. I mean, sure, I didn't want to think about it. But I guess also I didn't think anyone else would care much. That it'd be just a joke to them.

But when I say this to Eliza, she shakes her head. 'Look, I know I said that everyone thinks you're weird but I was wrong. Okay, you're different, but *good* different. You should've heard Leo raving on about you the other day. How cool it was that you were organising another rally and how we should definitely go this time.' Eliza grins at me. 'I think Hazel got a bit jealous, actually.'

'Ha!' I laugh back. 'As if. Anyway, he's not my type.'

The image of Josh flashes into my mind. The way he looked at me when we found the second note. I haven't told him yet about seeing Mrs Brinkman but he might know anyway. Anya is not the best at keeping secrets.

'I guess I just wanted to say that if anything like that happens again, tell me, okay?' says Eliza. 'I mean, I'm a bit older so I might be able to help you out. You know – like a big sister or whatever.' She says it in this very no-big-deal way, but I can tell she really means it.

I say, 'Thanks, I will,' in the same style. But I really mean it too.

Eleven

The next morning when I get up, Eliza has already gone. I feel my stomach drop a little. It would've been nice turning up at school with her instead of going by myself. I'm pretty sure people will have heard about the notes on my locker, and I'm worried everyone will stare at me. But it can't be helped, I guess.

Thomas and Oscar seem to be extra lively this morning, running around, yelling and jumping off things as I make the porridge.

Daphne shakes her head and smiles at me. 'You must

be looking forward to getting back to your nice, quiet, organised home tomorrow,' she says.

'A bit,' I say, laughing as Thomas rushes past making a steam train noise. There *are* things about home that I'm looking forward to – my comfy bed and seeing my parents again, and getting some help with Poss from Mum. But I'm going to miss being here with the Mitchells too.

'Okay, everyone,' says Daphne after breakfast. 'It's time to go. I'll meet you at the car in ten minutes.'

Riding in the car is something I *won't* miss, I think, as I go and brush my teeth. I wonder how my parents will react when I break the news that my bike has been stolen. Will I get in trouble for not bothering to lock it up?

Usually in the mornings I have to herd the boys out the door. There are always about fifteen things they *have* to do first – like finish their Lego creation or see if they can squeeze between the sofa and the wall. But today they're the ones dragging me out. 'Come on, Sophie,' Thomas keeps saying. 'We'll be late!'

When I open the front door, I see Daphne standing there with a bike. A beautiful green one, with a big red bow tied to the handlebars.

The boys go nuts. 'Surprise! Surprise!' they yell. 'We got you a bike!'

'I felt so bad about your bike being pinched from our yard,' Daphne explains. 'I remembered you said you liked green so I thought this might be okay.'

The bike is way more than okay. It is gorgeously, perfectly amazing. And it's absolutely, definitely *me*. I look at it longingly. Because there's a problem. 'There's no way Mum and Dad will let me take it.'

'Oh, but you *must* take it!' says Daphne earnestly. 'Your parents are part of the reason I got it. They've done so many nice things for me since we moved here – helped me out, given me things, fixed stuff. But they never accept anything in return. And it's second-hand, Soph. It wasn't expensive, I promise.'

The bike doesn't *look* second-hand. And I also start to wonder if maybe my old bike wasn't stolen at all. Maybe Daphne has hidden it somewhere – like in the shed out the back.

The boys start chanting, '*Try the bike! Try the bike!*'

Eventually I give in. 'Okay, okay! I'll try it! For today at least – until my parents say I have to give it back.'

'They won't say that,' says Daphne confidently.

The bike is light and comfortable to sit on. No squeaks. No swirls, no ribbons on the handlebars. I know what my mum would say. *It looks so ordinary. You'll just blend in with the crowd.* But that's exactly what I love about it. Surely it's okay to blend in sometimes? I ride off down the street with the two boys yelling and waving from the footpath.

V

When I get to school, no-one's around. Not Anya or Leni, not Josh or Adam. Not even Erin. It's weird. I mean, Anya is often late anyway, and maybe Leni had some extra training to do today, but it's strange that *none* of them are here. I have to face the long walk to homeroom on my own. Just as I feared, it feels like everyone is looking at me and whispering. Like they all know what happened. Maybe they think what Nelson wrote in the note was true and the picture of me was funny. That I'm a troublemaker and a weirdo and that I deserved it.

When I'm right near the lockers my heart almost stops. Because my locker is covered with folded pieces of paper, each with my name written across it, each in different handwriting. There are so many that when someone walks by, they all flutter like butterflies. Now I'm *sure* everyone is staring at me. Staring and waiting to see what I'll do. How I'll react. I can't move. My feet are stuck to the ground.

Then Leni appears from somewhere and gives me a little push towards the locker. 'It's okay, Soph,' she says. 'Go and have a look.' I force myself to walk up to the notes. I randomly pull one down. My hand shakes as I open it.

Dear Sophie,

You tell the truth when other people don't. You are a good listener too. It took us a while to get to know each other but I'm glad we did.

It's from Eliza, who I've now spotted grinning at me among the group of people now hanging by my locker.

Anya emerges from the crowd and comes up beside me.

'Read mine,' she says, pointing to a note that's covered in tiny, glittery hearts.

Dear Soph,

You are AMAZING! So strong and so brave and clever. But you don't have to be strong all the time. Leni and I are always there when you need us.

Love Anya.

I give Anya a hug. 'Thanks,' I say. 'I won't forget.'

Leni's note says:

You don't just believe what other people believe. You question stuff. I think that's great.

The crowd around my locker is growing. Some of the people I know, some I've never even spoken to. Leo is there with Hazel and when I look back to my locker, I spot a note where my name has been written like a grafitti tag. Inside is a drawing – a girl with long, wavy hair like mine. She has one hand stretched up into the air, and balanced on top is what I first think is a basketball, but then realise is a globe of the world. In the other hand, she's holding a sword.

Anya looks over my shoulder and laughs. 'Hey! She looks *just like* you! That must be Leo's note. Do you know he's also painted the ...'

Leni frowns at Anya and cuts her off. 'Keep reading the notes, Soph,' she says. 'You've got a lot to get through before the bell goes.'

I read solidly for ten minutes but it's hard to keep up. Just as I take one down, someone else will turn up and stick another on. I look at Leni and Anya and shake my head in amazement. 'How did you guys organise this?'

'Actually it was mostly Eliza,' says Anya. 'And when people found out about what Nelson did, they wanted you to know that not everyone thought like that.'

The bell has just rung when Adam and Josh appear, carrying a piece of folded cardboard about the size of a door. They lean the cardboard against my locker and Adam fastens it with a long bit of tape. Inside it says, *Sophie Bennett, you rock!*

Leni looks at Adam and raises her eyebrow. 'Big idea, few words, huh?'

'Something like that,' grins Adam.

I feel a whole lot of things right then, all mixed up into one. I'm embarrassed about the fuss and it's a bit horrible that everyone obviously knows what happened. But of course I'm also touched that so many people would do this for me. Even people I don't really know. In the notes, a lot of the same words keep popping up. *Admire. Respect. Strong. Brave*. They're good words. Words that I didn't realise people connected with me.

I guess you can be confused about who *you* really are, but you can also be totally confused – even wrong – about who other people are, too.

Everyone is heading off to class when Josh comes up and slips one more note in my hand. He looks a little red. 'The big note was really from Adam,' he says in a rush. 'This one is mine.'

'Thanks,' I say and suddenly my face feels hot too. I start to open it but he stops me.

'Uh, read it later,' he says and then he hurries away.

I try to make myself wait until the break to read Josh's note. But I can't hold out that long. I take a peek at it during class when no-one is looking.

Dear Soph,

How many other people would touch a dead possum to save its baby? How many other people give up their free time to fight for stuff they believe in? How many other people think as hard about things as you do?

I only know one. You.

Sophie, you are the coolest person I know. See you at the rally on Saturday.

This feeling, like the warmest of hugs, covers me. It takes a *lot* of effort not to start laughing right there in the middle of class. I manage it – just – but there's no way I can wipe the huge, happy, goofy grin off my face.

Twelve

On Saturday morning, my parents call from the bus and say they're going to be late.

From the corner of my eye, I see Daphne waving her hands around, trying to get my attention. 'Hang on a minute, Mum,' I say.

'Tell them we'll meet them at the rally,' says Daphne. 'We're all going anyway.'

'You're going to the rally?' I say, unable to keep the surprise out of my voice.

Daphne nods. 'Eliza wants to go and I thought it'd be good for the boys.'

I pass this message on to Mum and she sounds as surprised as I am. 'Do you think she's serious about going?' she says.

'Yes, I think so.' I lower my voice. 'Mum. She's even wearing *flat shoes.*'

Mum laughs and I can tell that, like me, she didn't realise that Daphne even owned any flat shoes!

I was planning to leave Poss at home, but at the last minute I put her into her travel pouch. It seems only fair that she should come to a rally to save her home.

We catch the train into town and the boys, who don't go on trains much, are super excited to be on one, and very, very loud.

Eliza sticks her fingers in her ears and looks at me, groaning. 'Any chance I can come and hide out at your place?' she says. 'You know, when the noise levels get dangerously high at home?'

I laugh. 'Sure. Anytime.'

I'm amazed at how many people have turned out for the rally. Sometimes there's hardly anyone at these things and that can be really depressing. But when there's lots of people you get this fantastic feeling – a '*great energy*' as my mum would say. Today the energy is incredible.

I find myself looking at other people and wondering about who they are and why they've come. You see such a mix of people at rallies – not just people like my parents. I love that. It makes you feel less alone, I guess. Like you're not the only one who cares about the planet. Like you don't have to save it all on your own.

'Sophie! Over here!'

I turn to see Anya waving at me like a mad thing. Beside her are Leni and Adam. Josh is there too. He grins at me and I grin back. The 'like' gauge has disappeared from my head, which is fine because I don't need it anymore. His note made it pretty clear how he feels. I'm about to go over and join my friends when someone taps me on the shoulder. It's Mrs Franks with her husband, and a little kid in a pusher.

'Mrs Franks!' I say. 'What are *you* doing here?'

She laughs. 'Because I want to save the forest, of course!'

'We used to like hiking there,' her husband adds. 'We're hoping we can do it again once Lucy's a bit bigger.'

Mrs Franks introduces me to her husband and he beams when he hears my name. 'So *you're* the famous Sophie Bennett!' he says. 'I've heard a lot about you.'

Anya comes over and tugs me away. 'Erin and George are here with the banner,' she says. 'You've *got* to come and see it.'

I'm dying to see the banner, actually. The others finished it yesterday at lunchtime, but I wasn't allowed in because it was a big surprise.

George and Erin unfurl it. 'Ta-dah!' says Erin.

Painted on it is a big portrait of Poss, based on the photo that Jo took. Underneath the picture it says, *Save my home.* The whole thing looks incredible.

'Leo did the outline for us,' Leni explains, 'and we coloured it in. Do you like it?'

I nod. 'I *love* it.'

As we raise up the banner, Poss pokes her head out of the pouch like she wants everyone to know that it's *her* in the portrait. It's super cute and people start pointing us out to each other and smiling.

A woman comes up with a huge camera and asks if she can take a photo. It turns out she works for the local newspaper and she's doing a story about the rally. We all crowd together and the photographer snaps away. She wants to know where we're from and why we're there.

Erin puts an arm around my shoulder. 'We're here because of Sophie,' she says.

The photographer turns to me. 'And why are *you* here?' she asks.

I think about it. I guess I could say I'm here because of my mum and dad. Or because it's just something I've always done. But these answers don't feel quite right. In the end I point down at Poss and say, 'I'm here because of her. When she's big enough, I want to release her into that forest. I want her to have a good place to live.'

My parents turn up just as the rally is about to start moving. I'm holding one side of the banner so I quickly pass it on to Anya and then I fling myself on them (being careful not to squash poor Poss, of course!). It's only been a few days since I saw them, but it feels like ages. I can tell they feel the same.

'You've grown!' my mum says.

'Who? Me or Poss?' I say.

Mum laughs. 'Both of you.'

'Looks like we're moving,' says Dad, and sure enough the crowd has started to walk.

'Are you going to walk with us, Soph?' asks Mum. 'Or with your friends?'

I look over to our rally group. More people have turned up now. Leo, Archie and all their skater friends. Hazel, Olympia, even Edi. Erin's friends Briana and Phoebe are standing with her and George, and Erin is trying to get them all chanting, *'We need trees! We need trees!'*

This *feeling* wells up inside me. This is amazing. All these people who could be doing something else, but they've decided to come here because they think this is worth fighting for. In the end, our Powerpoint presentation at assembly was just the big picture that Jo took of Poss and me blathering on for a bit. But maybe that was enough. Or maybe they were all planning on coming anyway. Whatever the reason, it makes me feel great.

And then there's Josh. I know he's there because he cares about this cause. But I think – I'm pretty sure, at least – that he's also here because of me.

I give my parents a hug. 'I might walk with my friends for a while,' I say.

The rally starts snaking its way down the main street. The trams can't go anywhere and people stare out the windows at us. Some people look annoyed, but other people are interested. They stop to watch and I even see a couple step off the road and join us, just for a block or two.

It's very crowded. So crowded that I don't think anyone notices when Josh, who is beside me, takes hold of my hand as we walk along. He gives me a shy smile and I smile back. And suddenly I don't feel like I'm walking anymore. I feel like I'm floating.

GIRL
V
THE
WORLD

Because you've got to be strong to take it on.

GIRL V THE WORLD
Things I Don't Know
Meredith Badger

GIRL V THE WORLD
Invisible Me
Chrissie Keighery

GIRL V THE WORLD
How to Boost Your Profile
Meredith Badger

GIRL V THE WORLD
Holy Crushamoly
Thalia Kalkipsakis